REDS

Two men, both in Russian military uniforms, one armed with a holstered pistol, the other with a machine gun—an AK-47, if Hickok remembered the gun manuals in the Family library correctly—appeared at the end of the corridor. They reacted to his presence instantly, the one with the pistol grabbing for his holster and the other soldier sweeping his AK-47 up.

Hickok was 30 feet from them. He never broke his stride as he leveled the Colts and fired, both Pythons booming simultaneously.

The two soldiers each took a slug between the eyes. The one with the pistol simply fell forward, but the trooper with the AK-47 tottered backwards, crashed into the left-hand wall, and dropped.

Hickok slowed as he neared the soldiers. He holstered the Colts and leaned over the soldier with the AK-47. "I need this more than you do."

Also in the ENDWORLD Series:

THE FOX RUN
THIEF RIVER FALLS RUN
TWIN CITIES RUN
KALISPELL RUN
DAKOTA RUN
CITADEL RUN
ARMAGEDDON RUN
DENVER RUN

DAVID ROBBINS
ENDWORLD
CAPITAL RUN

LEISURE BOOKS　　NEW YORK CITY

A LEISURE BOOK

Published by

Dorchester Publishing Co., Inc.
6 East 39th Street
New York, NY 10019

Copyright©1988 by David Robbins

All rights reserved. No part of this book may be reproduced or transmitted in any form or by any electronic or mechanical means, including photocopying, recording, or by any information storage and retrieval system, without the written permission of the Publisher, except where permitted by law.

Printed in the United States of America

1

The two women were fleeing for their lives.

They raced over the crest of a low hill, the statuesque redhead and the petite brunette, their legs churning, sweat caking their skin, their breathing labored as their straining lungs gasped for air. The redhead was in the lead, a few feet in front of her companion. Both women wore similar black-leather outfits consisting of a tight vest and skimpy shorts, appropriate attire considering the heat of the June day and their strenuous exertion.

"We'll never make it!" the brunette cried, wheezing.

The redhead glanced over her right shoulder and scowled. "We'll make it, damnit! Don't give up on me now!"

"I'm doing the best I can, Lexine," the brunette stated.

Lexine smiled encouragingly. "Hang in there, Mira," she said, her tone reflecting her concern for her friend. "Another mile and we'll take to the trees."

The duo jogged onward, sticking to the center of the highway, carefully avoiding the dozens of potholes and deep ruts pockmarking the ancient asphalt surface.

Mira stumbled and almost fell.

Lexine slowed and grabbed Mira's right hand, supporting her. "Lean on me," she offered.

Mira shook her head, her short hair bobbing. "I'd

only slow you down."

"Don't worry about it," Lexine said.

"Maybe we should take to the trees now," Mira suggested.

Both sides of the highway were lined with dense vegetation, affording ample hiding space and shelter from the sweltering temperature.

"We've got to put as much distance between them and us as we can," Lexine declared. "This way is faster."

Mira panted as she struggled to stay abreast of Lexine. "I don't like being out in the open like this!" she remarked. "At least in the woods they wouldn't find us."

"Don't forget the dogs," Lexine reminded the brunette.

Mira blanched and increased her speed.

Minutes passed in relative quiet, broken by the pounding of their leather sandals on the roadway and the ragged sound of their breathing.

"You know this is crazy, don't you?" Mira asked.

"Save your energy," Lexine said.

"We'll never make it!" Mira reiterated.

From behind them, in the distance, came a peculiar buzzing.

Mira slowed, cocking her head. "Do you hear it?" she wailed.

Lexine stopped and turned, her shoulder-length hair whipping around her neck. "I hear them," she confirmed.

"Dear God! What do we do?" Mira almost screamed, panic contorting her narrow features.

Lexine glared at her friend, her green eyes blazing. "Get a grip on yourself!" she commanded.

The strange buzzing was becoming louder and louder.

"They're going to catch up!" Mira whined.

Lexine pointed to their left. "Into the trees. Move!"

Mira shuffled toward the woods, her brown eyes wide, staring at the hill to their rear.

Lexine moved to the left, her right hand gripping the handle of the 15-inch survival knife attached by its brown sheath to her black belt, just above her right hip. If they were caught, she told herself, she would give a good accounting for her life! She wouldn't be wasted without a fight! But maybe they wouldn't be caught. If they could only reach the trees and take cover, there was a good chance Cardew and the others would pass them by.

If they could only reach those trees!

Lexine was a yard from the edge of the highway when she heard a sharp screech followed by the dull thud of a body slamming to the pavement. She whirled, knowing what she would see.

Mira had tripped in a pothole and fallen onto her stomach, scraping her knees and elbows in the process.

Lexine hurried to her friend and took hold of her left elbow. "On your feet!" she snapped. "We've got to reach the woods!"

Mira, moaning, rose to a crouching position. "My right leg feels like it's broken!" she wailed.

"It's not broken!" Lexine disputed, well aware of Mira's propensity for exaggeration. "Now move your ass!"

Mira abruptly straightened, forgetting all about her "broken" leg. "Look!" she screamed. "It's them!"

Lexine spun.

There were four of them poised on the crown of the hill, their cycles idling, their black-leather jackets and pants lending an ominous aspect to their appearance.

"Damn!" Lexine fumed. Why the hell had she ever agreed to bring Mira along? Mira wasn't up to this. She had slowed them down, and now they were as good as dead.

"Here they come!" Mira shrieked.

The four riders gunned their motorcycles and roared down the hill, zooming toward the two women.

Lexine drew her knife and stepped in front of Mira, her countenance grim, her determination revealed in the compressed line of her red lips and the jutting set of her pointed chin.

The motorcycles closed in. Three of the riders were women, the fourth a tall man. His dark hair, dyed blue, was shaped in a Mohawk, the exposed skin on either side of his mane of hair tanned a deep brown by the scorching sun. A chain belt secured his leather pants. Attached to the belt above his right hip was a brown holster containing a Browning Hi-Power 9-mm Auto Pistol.

Lexine warily watched the approaching bikers, wishing she had a gun of her own.

The three women bikers all wore black leather, and only one of them was armed with a handgun, a Charter Arms Bulldog in a shoulder holster under her left arm. The other two women were each packing a knife and a sword. One of them, a blonde, wore her knife on her left hip, while the other wore the knife on her right. Both women carried their swords in leather scabbards strapped to their backs.

"What do we do?" Mira wanted to know.

Lexine didn't answer. There was nothing they could do.

The man with the Mohawk braked his big Harley to a stop not ten feet in front of them. The woman with the Bulldog slid to a halt six feet to their right, the blonde did likewise to their left, and the final woman circled and stopped about eight feet behind them.

Lexine frowned. They were surrounded.

All four switched off their bikes at the same moment. The resultant silence, after the rumbling clamor of the cycles, seemed unnatural.

Lexine detected a slight ringing in her ears.

Mohawk grinned, displaying a gap where two of his

upper front teeth had once been, and leaned back on his Harley. "Well, well, well," he said sarcarstically, winking at the blonde. "What do we have here?"

The blonde snickered. "It's big, bad Lex and her shadow, Mira the wimp."

"Who are you calling a wimp?" Mira demanded defensively.

The blonde glanced at Mohawk. "Mira is all mine," she told him.

"Whatever you want, Pat," Mohawk said.

Lexine snorted. "How do you stand it, Cardew?" she asked the male biker.

"Stand what?" Cardew responded.

"That brown stain coating your nose," Lexine stated.

Cardew laughed at her insult. "I always did like your sense of humor, Lex. I'm going to miss it."

"Just like that, huh?" Lexine said.

"Yep. Just like that. I have my orders," Cardew informed her. "Terza was real clear on what she wants done with you."

"I'll bet she was," Lexine snapped.

Cardew sighed and shook his head. "You knew this was coming, Lex. No one defies Terza. You know that."

"Let's get this over with!" Pat interjected. "Let's waste these dumb bitches and head back."

Lexine faced the blonde. "You talk real brave when the odds are four to two. But how are you when it's one on one?"

Pat scowled. "You think you can take me?"

Lexine nodded, her green eyes twinkling. "I know I can take you."

"We'll see about that!" Pat slammed her kickstand down and climbed from her Triumph.

"What are you doing?" Cardew asked her.

"What does it look like I'm doing?" Pat retorted.

"Terza said we're to make it quick," Cardew said.

"I'll make it quick," Pat promised. She smiled and slowly drew her sword.

"Cut Lex to ribbons!" urged the woman with the Bulldog.

"Don't worry," Pat said. "I will."

Lexine moved to her right, keeping her eyes on that sword. It had a 30-inch double-edged blade and a large hilt, and it had been especially crafted for Pat by one of the blacksmiths.

Pat, confident in her ability and the superior reach of her weapon, walked directly toward the redhead. "I'm going to take your head back to Terza as a gift."

"Come and get it," Lexine said, baiting her adversary.

Pat charged, swinging her sword in a wide arc.

Lexine quickly ducked and dodged to her right, avoiding the gleaming sword.

Pat swung again, drawing nearer, aiming an overhead swipe at Lexine's head.

Lexine parried the sword with her survival knife, the blades clanging as they struck.

The blonde brought her sword around again.

Lexine managed to deflect the blade with her knife as she deftly slide aside, darting to the left.

"Lexine!" Mira cried in alarm.

Without warning, before Lexine could fathom her intent, Pat turned and took three steps, her arms upraised, the sword clasped with the blade upright, only a foot from Mira.

"No!" Lexine shouted.

Mira, too terrified to react, flinched as the sword flashed downward.

Lexine, shocked to her core, saw the sword cleave Mira's face, splitting it from the forehead to the chin.

Mira stiffened and gurgled as Pat withdrew her blade. A crimson flood poured from the wound as Mira sagged to the ground.

"*No!*" Enraged, Lexine leaped at the blonde. She

stabbed and slashed in a frenzied fury, but Pat was able to block or counter every blow. Heedless of her safety, Lexine pressed her attack. She forced the blonde to retreat several paces. Eager to bury her knife in Pat's chest, she gambled on a desperate lunge.

Pat easily sidestepped.

Lexine felt her right foot catch in one of the deep cracks in the road and she stumbled forward, unable to regain her balance. Her left knee smashed onto the asphalt. She frantically struggled to rise, to confront her foe, fearing Pat would plunge the sword into her exposed back.

But nothing happened.

Lexine rose and turned, her knife at the ready.

Pat was only three feet away, but she wasn't looking at Lexine. Neither were Cardew or the other two women.

What in the world? Astonished, Lexine glanced in the direction they were staring, to the west. That's when she saw him.

The stranger. Calmly standing in the middle of the road, not ten feet away, he was a wiry, diminutive man dressed in black. His features were handsomely Oriental, his eyes and hair dark. A long, black scabbard was clutched in his left hand.

Lexine had never seen a man like this newcomer. There was an unusual quality about the man, a visible air of supreme self-confidence combined with a palpable aura of inner strength. His expression exhibited an inherent honesty and fearlessness. Lexine experienced a stirring deep within her, a reaction to the stranger's mere presence. Unlike the servile men in the Leather Knights, she intuitively sensed that here, at last, was a *real* man.

Cardew was the first to recover his voice. "Who the hell are you?" he demanded, his right hand inching toward his Browning Auto Pistol.

"I am called Rikki," the newcomer replied in a soft, low voice.

"Where did you come from?" Cardew angrily demanded, scanning the vegetation on both sides of the road.

"My body came from my mother's womb," the stranger said quietly. "My spirit came from the Eternal Source of all life."

Lexine almost laughed at the ludicrous contours on Cardew's face as his mouth dropped open in amazement.

Pat walked toward the newcomer, cautiously extending her sword. "Cut the crap, jerk! We want some answers and we want them now!"

"I have supplied the proper answers," the stranger stated.

"Maybe we should take this bozo back to Terza," Cardew suggested nervously.

"I am not going anywhere?" the man in black said.

"Wanna bet?" Pat countered.

"I do not gamble," the newcomer told her.

"Is this guy for real?" asked the woman with the Bulldog. Her right hand was resting on the revolver.

Pat stopped a yard from the stranger. "We want to know where you came from," she reiterated, "and we want to know right now."

Lexine saw the man in black gaze at Pat. Surprisingly, Pat backed up a step—surprising because Lexine had never seen Pat back down from anyone or anything.

The newcomer shifted his attention to Lexine. "I do not understand the reason for your conflict, but I do not believe four against one are honorable odds. Would you care for my assistance?"

Pat moved forward again before Lexine could respond. "Who the hell do you think you are? This is a private matter."

The man in black locked his dark eyes on Pat. "Not

any more," he said, accenting each word.

Something seemed to snap inside of Pat. "Damn you!" she bellowed, and aimed a swipe at the stranger.

Lexine could scarcely believe what transpired next. In her 23 years she had participated in dozens of fights and witnessed dozens more, savage engagements, life-or-death exchanges conducted by men and women skilled in the many arts of combat. She had seen swordsmen and swordswomen of consummate proficiency. But not one of them had come close to matching the lightning speed of the man in black.

The stranger called Rikki twisted slightly, and his right hand was a streak as he drew his sword. The stroke was impossible to see; one moment he was drawing his sword, and in the next instant Pat had frozen in her tracks, her head flopping backward, nearly decapitated, a shred of skin and her upper spinal column all that remained of her neck.

Cardew and the other two women went for their weapons.

Lexine saw the man in black drop his scabbard, his left hand reaching behind his back and emerging with an odd metal star clasped in his fingers. His left arm swept up and out.

The biker on Lexine's right was drawing the Bulldog, the revolver clear of its shoulder holster and leveling when the metal star arced across the intervening space and imbedded itself in her forehead. The woman with the Bulldog jerked in her seat, her eyes widening in disbelief. She gasped and began to slide to the ground.

The third woman biker was drawing her sword when the man in black took two rapid steps and plunged his blade into her throat.

Lexine abruptly realized they were still in danger and spun to confront Cardew.

The Harley roared to life even as Lexine turned,

and before she could reach him Cardew gunned his bike and executed a tight U-turn, heading east, his motorcycle accelerating rapidly. Within seconds, he passed over the crest of the low hill and vanished.

"Now we know who the real wimp is," Lexine said aloud. She stared sadly at Mira, then looked at the three other dead women lying sprawled on the highway.

The man in black wiped his sword clean on Pat's vest, then crossed to the woman with the Bulldog. He leaned over and extracted his metal star from her forehead, wiping it on the woman's leather pants.

"What is that thing?" Lexine asked. "I've never seen anything like it."

The stranger slid the star into a brown pouch attached to his belt, positioned in the small of his back. "It is called a shuriken," he informed her.

"You're real good with that shuriken," Lexine said, complimenting him.

He retrieved his scabbard and carefully slid the sword inside.

"I've never seen a sword like yours either," Lexine commented.

The man hefted his weapon. "This is my katana. It was constructed centuries ago by a master metalsmith in Japan."

"Where's Japan?" Lexine inquired.

The man in black studied her.

"What did you say your name was again?" Lexine probed when he continued to scrutinize her. His examination made her feel uncomfortable; she entertained the ridiculous notion he could see into her inner being.

"I am Rikki-Tikki-Tavi," he stated.

Lexine chuckled. "That's a weird name. Where'd your parents ever get a name like that?"

"My parents did not bestow it on me," Rikki said. "I selected it at my Naming."

"Let me get this straight," Lexine remarked. "You picked your own name?"

Rikki nodded. "It is a common practice where I come from. The man responsible for starting our Family wanted us to go through our vast library and select whatever name we liked for our own."

"Why?"

Rikki glanced at the four bodies. "We can discuss this in depth later. I must report this incident immediately. You are welcome to come with me if you desire."

Lexine gazed at Mira. "Don't mind if I do. Nothing's holding me here."

"Do you want your friend buried?" Rikki queried her.

Lexine frowned and shook her head. "Nope. Let the buzzards have her. We'd best make tracks."

"What is your name?" Rikki asked.

Lexine tore her eyes from Mira. "Oh. I didn't tell you, did I? I'm Lexine. But all my friends call me Lex."

"Tell me, Lexine—" Rikki began.

"It's Lex," she quickly corrected him.

The corners of his thin lips twisted upward. "Tell me, Lex, will the one who escaped return with others?"

Lex looked at the hill to the east. "Most likely. Terza will want your hide after what you did to three of her Knights. And they want me for trying to skip."

Rikki pointed to the west. "Are you up to some running?"

"Try me," Lex said gamely.

They began jogging westward down the middle of the highway, side by side. Lex found herself surreptitiously admiring Rikki's firm features and his lithe, easy stride.

"Are we far from St. Louis?" he unexpectedly asked her.

"Nope," Lex responded. "St. Louis is about seven miles to the east. That's where I came from."

"Why were you leaving?"

Lex glowered. "I want to live my own life. There has to be something better than the Leather Knights."

"What are the Leather Knights?"

Lex glanced down at him. "You sure aren't from around these parts. Everybody knows about the Leather Knights. They run St. Louis."

"You mean they control the city?" Rikki asked.

"They own the turf," she clarified for him.

"Are you a Leather Knight?"

"I was," Lex admitted. "But not any more. Now I'm just a traitor to them. They'll waste me if they get their paws on me again."

Rikki looked up into her green eyes. She was at least ten inches taller than him. "We'll have to see to it they don't."

Lex, for one of the few times in her life, blushed, a pink tinge capping her rounded cheeks.

"Tell me about these Leather Knights," Rikki urged her.

"What's to tell?" Lex replied. "There's about four hundred Leather Knights. And there's about two hundred studs. That—"

"Studs?" Rikki interrupted.

"Yeah. The auxiliaries. Each one takes the oath before they get their bike, same as the regular Leather Knights, but of course they don't have the same privileges."

"You take an oath?"

"Of course. That's why my life is on the line. We take an oath, a blood oath, to always obey the code of the Leather Knights." Lex sighed. "Anyone who betrays it is automatically sentenced to death."

"They won't even permit you to leave?" Rikki inquired.

Lex shook her head, her red hair flying. "Not on

your life. When you take the Leather Knight oath, you're a Knight forever."

"And every Leather Knight receives a motorcycle?"

"Yep. They . . ." Lex abruptly stopped. "Damn! What an idiot I am!"

Rikki halted and faced her. "What's the matter?"

Lex pointed at the bodies and the three abandoned bikes, now 50 yards distant. "Why didn't we take one of their bikes?" she demanded.

Rikki shrugged. "It never occurred to me. I don't know how to drive one."

"Well I do!" Lex exclaimed, annoyed at her stupidity. Why hadn't she thought of it? Probably because she was too busy thinking of him.

Rikki gazed westward. "I have some friends about a mile down the road. Perhaps we should use one of those cycles. We would reach them faster."

"The faster, the better," Lex agreed.

They started running back toward the cycles.

"You say you've never ridden a bike before?" Lex asked.

"No. I've seen photographs of them in books in the Family library, but I've never ridden one," Rikki stated.

"Then you're in for a treat," Lex said. "Riding a bike is the second best feeling I know."

"What's the first?" Rikki innocently queried.

Lex shot him a puzzled look. "You're putting me on, right?"

Now it was Rikki's turn to appear perplexed. "No," he assured her.

Lex laughed. "You really are weird, aren't you?"

They ran in silence for several moments.

"Did you hear that?" Rikki asked.

"Hear what?"

"That."

From the east, from the other side of the hill, rose

an eerie howling.

"Son of a bitch!" Lex blurted.

"What is it?"

"The dogs," Lex answered anxiously. "The three you wasted and the dummy who got away were probably the advance riders from a hunting party. That dummy, Cardew, must have reached them and they've sicced the dogs on us!"

The howling grew in volume and intensity.

"There must be at least a dozen," Rikki speculated.

"They'll tear us apart," Lex said.

"Not if I can help it," Rikki vowed.

They were 20 yards from the bikes when the dog pack appeared on the hill to the east. At the sight of the two people below, their intended quarry, the pack burst into a refrain of baying and barking. Galvanized by the sight of their prey, the dogs loped down the hill and raced toward the man and woman.

Rikki counted 16 dogs, all of them large and mean, the pack consisting mainly of German shepherds and Dobermans.

Lexine, her long legs flying toward the cycles, was mentally berating herself for her dumb behavior. Not only had she completely overlooked the possibility of using one of the bikes, but she'd also neglected to retrieve the Charter Arms Bulldog from the biker Rikki had killed with the shuriken. She had to get a grip on her emotions. Sure, she found the little guy exceptionally attractive, but that didn't excuse her mistakes, not when those mistakes could wind up costing her life.

The dogs were covering the ground in a feral rush. Two of them, a dusky shepherd and an ebony Doberman, were 15 feet in front of the pack and closing at an astonishing clip.

We'll never make it! Lexine told herself. She reached the first cycle and grabbed the handlebars even as Rikki swept past her, his katana drawn and held in his right hand, his scabbard in his left.

The dogs never hesitated. The German shepherd and the Doberman ignored the bodies on the road and bounded toward the man in black.

Rikki took out the Doberman, the closest one, first, his katana a gleaming blur as he sliced the canine open from its chin to its sternum. He twisted, avoiding the hurtling Doberman and concentrating on the shepherd. Several seconds were required before the Doberman realized the gravity of its wound. It twirled, preparing for another attack, when its front paws slipped on a moist substance coating the highway and it fell. Vertigo overwhelmed it, and the Doberman watched helplessly as the man in black hacked off the top of the shepherd's head with his flashing sword.

"Look out!" Lex screamed.

Rikki barely had time to brace himself before the rest of the pack was on them. He dropped his scabbard and assumed chudan-no-kumae.

2

"He should have been back by now, pard."

"We'll give him a little while yet."

"Whatever you want. I've just got a bad feeling, is all," said the first speaker, a lean, blond man with long hair and a drooping mustache dressed in buckskins and moccasins. Strapped around his narrow waist were twin holsters containing a pair of pearl-handled Colt Python revolvers. The fringe on his buckskin shirt stirred in the afternoon breeze as he glanced at his traveling companion. "I reckon we should check on him, Blade."

The other man slowly nodded. He was a towering giant, a powerhouse with an awesome physique and bulging muscles. His wardrobe consisted of a black-leather vest, green fatigue pants, and black boots. On each huge hip, snug in its respective sheath, was a Bowie knife. Slung over his left shoulder was a Commando Arms Carbine with a 90-shot magazine, modified to full automatic by the Family Gunsmiths. His dark hair and eyes lent a grim, somber aspect to his appearance. "Maybe you're right, Hickok," Blade said to the gunman. "Rikki was only supposed to scout ahead for a mile or two. According to the maps, we're almost to the outskirts of St. Louis. Whether he saw any sign of the city or not, he should have been back by now."

"I just hope he didn't go and get into a fix," Hickok griped. "I want to get this assignment over with and return to the Home."

"You didn't need to come along," Blade reminded him. "This was a volunteer mission. You knew that."

"Yeah," Hickok said wistfully. "When Plato first announced it, I figured I could use the break. Get out of the cabin for a spell. Break the monotony. You know what I mean?"

Blade nodded.

"But I miss 'em," Hickok said sadly. "I miss Sherry and my son. Little Ringo," he stated proudly. "I want to see 'em both so bad."

"I know how you feel," Blade assured the gunfighter. "I miss my wife and boy too."

"Where the blazes is Rikki?" Hickok snapped impatiently.

Blade gazed to the east, reflecting, recalling the day only three months before when the Leader of the Family, Plato, had called all of them together in the walled compound designated their Home, located in the extreme northwest of Minnesota. "We require volunteers from the Warrior ranks," Plato had informed them. "As you know, we have established peaceful relations with the Flathead Indians in Montana, with the horsemen known as the Cavalry in the Dakota Territory, and with what's left of the U.S. Government to the west and south, in the Civilized Zone. We're also friendly with the refugees from the Twin Cities now living near us, and with the Moles to our east. But we are ignorant of what exists west of the Rocky Mountains and east of the Mississippi River. Consequently, the leaders of the various groups I've mentioned, which we now collectively refer to as the Freedom Federation, have decided to send an expedition into uncharted land, to venture where none of us have gone in one hundred years. We've heard many terrifying rumors about the country east of the Mississippi. We must determine if the rumors are true or mere fabrications. It is imperative we

learn if there is any danger to our Family and the
Freedom Federation as a whole. We now have fifteen
Warriors safeguarding our Home and preserving us
from harm. I propose to have the Warriors draw lots,
and the three drawing the shortest straws will make
the journey. Do you agree?'' Plato had asked.

Blade frowned at the memory. The Family had con-
curred with their leader, and Plato had held a
conference with the head of the Warriors. Blade,
despite his better judgment, had offered to lead the
expedition, to forgo drawing a lot. Plato had gladly
accepted his offer. The rest of the Warriors drew lots,
and Rikki-Tikki-Tavi and Geronimo had drawn the
shortest straws. But Geronimo's wife, Cynthia
Morning Dove, had given birth only a week before
the drawing. Hickok had therefore stepped forward
and volunteered to go in Geronimo's place, and Plato
had accepted the proposition after Geronimo had
reluctantly acquiesced.

So here I am, Blade told himself. Almost to St. Louis
and wishing I was anywhere but here. What a jerk I
was to agree to go! And all because I think I can drive
the SEAL better than anyone else in the Family, and
certainly better than any of the other Warriors.

The SEAL. The pride and joy of the Founder of the
Home, a man named Kurt Carpenter.

Carpenter had wisely anticipated the advent of
World War III. A wealthy filmmaker, he had devoted
his millions to constructing a survivalist retreat he
had dubbed the Home. Shortly before the outbreak of
hostilities, he had invited a carefully selected group to
the Home. Because the retreat was located hundreds
of miles from any primary, secondary, or even
tertiary targets, it was spared a direct hit. Thanks to
the prevailing high-altitude winds at the time of the
war, the Home received only minimal dosages of
radiation. Carpenter had planned for practically
every contingency. He'd stocked ample supplies of

every conceivable type.

His crowning achievement was the vehicle he bestowed on his followers, a vehicle he'd spent a fortune having developed. Carpenter had christened it the Solar Energized Amphibious or Land Recreational Vehicle—SEAL for short. The SEAL was a vanlike transport, green in color, with an impervious body composed of an indestructible plastic. The plastic was tinted, allowing those within to see out but preventing anyone outside from viewing the interior. Four enormous tires allowed the transport to navigate virtually any terrain. The SEAL received its power from a pair of solar panels attached to the roof, which in turn supplied converted energy to six revolutionary batteries mounted under the vehicle. As if all of this weren't enough, Carpenter had then hired skilled mercenaries to install special armaments in the SEAL. As far as Blade knew, there wasn't another vehicle like it on the entire planet. He abruptly became aware of Hickok speaking.

"—listening to me or am I flappin' my gums for the fun of it?" the gunman demanded.

"Sorry," Blade apologized. "What were you saying?"

Hickok chuckled. "I never realized how much you and my missus have in common," he quipped.

"What's that supposed to mean?" Blade inquired.

"It means you're both pretty darn good at ignoring me at times," Hickok said. "It must be my introverted personality."

"Yeah, right," Blade responded. "You're about as introverted as a bull elk during rutting season. What were you—"

Hickok suddenly held up his right hand for silence. "Shush, pard! Give a listen!"

Blade complied, his ears straining. "I don't hear

anything," he declared after several seconds.

"You'd best clean your ears out," Hickok cracked, then paused. "Now do you hear it?"

Blade did. A faint sound coming from the east. An odd noise. Sort of a soft whump-whump-whump. What could it be?

"There!" Hickok exclaimed, pointing. "See it?"

Blade saw it. About a mile off to the east, hovering in the air, a huge dragonfly-shaped object.

"What the blazes is it?" Hickok asked.

"I don't know," Blade admitted. He racked his brain, recalling all the hours spent in the huge Family library personally stocked by Kurt Carpenter. Hundreds of thousands of books on every conceivable subject: dozens upon dozens of how-to books for everything from woodworking to herbal remedies; history books; literature books; religion and philosophy books; photographic books depicting the state of civilization before World War III one hundred years ago; and many, many more. Several of the books were devoted to aviation, and one of the photographs came to mind as Blade watched the aircraft. "I think that thing is called a helicopter," he remarked.

"A helicopter?" Hickok repeated doubtfully. "Who would have a functional helicopter? Where did it come from?"

From far off, from the vicinity of the helicopter, came the sharp retort of gunfire.

Blade and Hickok exchanged worried glances.

"Rikki!" Hickok said apprehensively.

"We'd better check it out," Blade declared. He turned toward the SEAL, parked behind them in the center of the highway.

"Look!" Hickok cried. "That contraption is comin' our way!"

The helicopter was rapidly approaching them, apparently flying directly over the road, following the course of the highway.

Blade's hands dropped to his Bowies. As the craft neared, he could distinguish its features. The helicopter was a dull brown in color with some sort of glass or plastic bubble in the front section and a long metallic tail behind. There was a spinning rotor on top of the craft and another one attached to the rear. Long, metal legs were affixed horizontally to the underbelly of the helicopter.

"Orders?" Hickok asked.

The bubble on the helicopter was tinted, just like the body of the SEAL, preventing Blade from viewing the interior of the craft. He debated the wisdom of remaining in the open, of attempting to persuade the occupants to land, hoping they would be friendly.

"They're almost on us," Hickok said, stating the obvious.

What to do? Blade hesitated.

Without any warning, the helicopter abruptly opened up with its machine guns, belching death and destruction from a pair of 45-caliber guns mounted on the front of the craft.

"Look out!" Hickok shouted, diving to the right as the highway in front of them erupted in a violent spray of asphalt and dirt.

Blade leaped aside, sprawling onto the ground. Damn his idiocy! How could he forget his favorite motto! Better safe than sorry!

Several of the rounds struck the SEAL, whining as they ricocheted from its steely structure.

Blade rolled to his feet.

Hickok was already on, his Pythons out and angled. As the helicopter passed overhead he fired four times in swift succession.

The helicopter kept going, circling around for another strafing run.

"In the SEAL!" Blade commanded. He ran to the driver's door, yanked it open, and vaulted into the driver's seat.

Hickok holstered his Colts and clambered into the passenger side. "Dangblasted varmints!" he muttered as he slammed his door. "Do you reckon they got Rikki?"

"We'll check on Rikki after we take care of these bastards!" Blade promised.

The SEAL was hit again, the screeching of the heavy slugs as they were deflected by the bulletproof body almost painful to the ears.

The helicopter streaked overhead, swinging for another try.

"Let's take 'em!" Hickok said.

Blade turned the key in the ignition and the engine purred to life.

The interior of the SEAL had been designed with economy of space in mind. Two bucket seats were in the front, one for the driver and another for a passenger, separated by a console between them. Behind the bucket seats was a wide seat for additional passengers, while the rear section, embracing at least a third of the transport, was devoted to storage space. The Warriors had their food, spare ammunition, and other provisions stacked in the rear section.

Blade shifted into drive and plastered the accelerator to the floor. The SEAL surged forward.

"They're comin' straight at us!" Hickok yelled.

The helicopter gunner fired again.

Blade swerved to the left as the windshield was rocked by a sustained burst.

"Are those bozos in for a surprise!" Hickok predicted, his right hand resting on the dashboard next to four silver toggle switches.

The mercenaries Kurt Carpenter had employed were proficient at their craft. The SEAL incorporated four offensive armaments into its framework: a pair of 50-caliber machine guns mounted underneath each front headlight; a flamethrower positioned behind the front fender; a rocket launcher in the center of the front grill; and even a miniaturized surface-to-air missile secreted in the roof above the driver's seat.

Hickok's hand touched the toggle switch marked S. "Ready when you are, big guy."

Blade had lost sight of the helicopter. Keeping the SEAL at 50 miles an hour, he leaned down and craned his neck in an effort to locate their antagonist. "I can't see them," he said.

"So what?" Hickok replied. "This surface-to-air dingus is heat-seeking, isn't it? Just say the word and it will take care of the rest."

"I don't want to waste it," Blade stated. "I want to be sure."

Hickok peered out his side of the transport. "I see a starling up there. Do you want me to practice on it?"

"Find the copter!" Blade ordered.

A minute passed without another attack.

"Maybe they headed for the hills," Hickok said.

"We've got to be sure," Blade told the gunfighter.

The SEAL was heading east, toward St. Louis.

"Where do you think it came from?" Hickok absently queried.

"How would I know?" Blade retorted.

Hickok grinned. "Boy! Somebody tries to kill you and you go to pieces! It doesn't take much to put you in a bad mood, does it?"

Blade braked the transport. "Get the binoculars."

Hickok climbed over the console and the wide seat into the rear section. "Where the blazes did we put them?" he asked.

"They've got to be there somewhere," Blade said, still searching for the helicopter.

Hickok unexpectedly started coughing. "Oh no!" he cried in mock horror.

"What is it?" Blade demanded, turning in his seat.

Hickok was pinching his nose shut with his right hand while he held a pair of black socks aloft in his left. "I found your dirty socks!" He wheezed.

"Whew! How does Jenny stand it?" he asked, referring to Blade's wife.

Blade glared at this friend. "Forget the socks and find those binoculars!"

"We don't need them," Hickok said, dropping the smelly socks.

"Why not?"

"Look!" Hickok pointed out the passenger side of the SEAL.

Blade turned.

The helicopter was coming in from the south, angling for a broadside run.

In the fraction of a second before Blade reacted, he spotted a bright red star painted on the tail of the copter. He buried the accelerator and slewed the SEAL to the left, off the highway and into the trees, barreling through the brush and snapping limbs and small saplings as the transport plowed onward.

To their rear, a large portion of the road exploded skyward as a deafening blast rocked the countryside.

"They must have rockets!" Hickok exclaimed as he climbed over the center seat and the console and reached his bucket seat.

Blade stopped the SEAL under the spreading branches of a large maple tree. The vehicle's green color, he reasoned, would serve as excellent camouflage in the midst of the forest.

"Do you reckon those hombres lost us?" Hickok queried.

"Let's hope so," Blade answered.

"I still think we should have used the surface-to-air gizmo on those suckers!" Hickok said.

"If they come back we will," Blade pledged.

But the helicopter didn't return. The two Warriors waited and waited, their windows lowered, listening for the whirlybird.

"They must have skedaddled," Hickok speculated after a while.

"Maybe they were low on fuel," Blade guessed. He

had left the SEAL's engine idle while they waited, knowing there was no way the occupants of the aircraft could have heard its barely audible motor. Besides, he realized, he might need to make a hasty getaway.

"We'd best check on Rikki, pard," Hickok suggested.

"Yes, we'd better," Blade agreed. He carefully wheeled the transport between the trees and other vegetation as he executed a wide circle back to the highway. "He shouldn't be too far ahead."

"What if he heard the fireworks and came a-runnin'?" Hickok inquired. "That helicopter might have went after him."

"We would have heard it," Blade said. "What I want to know," he added thoughtfully, "is what was all that shooting we heard when we first saw the copter?"

The SEAL broke though the final row of trees and reached the highway, coming out into the open about 20 yards from the point where they entered.

"Did you see that red star?" Hickok asked.

"I saw it," Blade confirmed, driving east.

"What's it mean?" Hickok questioned.

"Beats me," Blade responded. "We'll have to study up on insignias after we return to the Home."

"If we return to our Home," Hickok mumbled.

"Nothing's going to prevent us from returning to our loved ones," Blade vowed.

As if on cue, the helicopter zipped into sight from the north. It hovered stationary for a moment directly in front of the SEAL. There was a puff of white smoke from the underbelly of the craft.

"They've fired a rocket!" Hickok shouted.

Blade could see the black rocket or missile hurtling toward the transport. There wasn't time to reach the safety of the woods again! And they certainly couldn't outrun it!

What else could they do?

3

Rikki-Tikki-Tavi's skills as a martial artist was renowned, the tales of his exploits matched or surpassed by only a few of the Warriors: Blade, Geronimo, Yama, and definitely Hickok. For years his deadly expertise as the consummate lethal perfectionist in hand-to-hand combat or with Oriental weaponry had been common knowledge among the Family in northwestern Minnesota. Later, when the Family and the other members of the Freedom Federation fought the demented Doktor in a battle dubbed Armageddon, and again when the Freedom Federation launched an assault on Denver, Rikki had demonstrated his prowess against human and bestial foes. True, the stories told about him had not attained the epic proportions of those told about Hickok, but in an age devoid of mass entertainment, when television and movies no longer fabricated false heroes for the populace, when the lost art of storytelling had regained its deserved prominence around countless campfires and dinner tables, the name of Rikki-Tikki-Tavi was one to be reckoned with. From northwestern Minnesota south to Texas, from Denver east to Kansas City, whenever people talked about the monumental clash between the Freedom Federation and the Civilized Zone, whenever the principles in that bloody, brutal conflict were mentioned, his name was high among them. And on this day Rikki lived up to his reputation.

Lexine drew her survival knife as the dog pack closed in. She backed against the motorcycle, hoping the bike would protect her flank while she concentrated on the dogs in front of her.

None of them reached her.

Rikki's katana was an invisible blur as he waded into the ferocious mass of canines. The first dog lost its front legs, the second half of its head, and the third was gutted in the twinkling of an eye. Rikki spun and slashed, twisted and sliced, constantly moving, his sharp-edged sword cleaving a foreleg here, a stomach there, or splitting a skull as easily as an overripe melon. The bravest dogs and the fleetest of foot were the first to die; eight went down in as many seconds, some gushing blood and howling in torment. Rikki's custom-made black clothing, especially sewn together by the Family Weavers, was spattered with crimson splotches and chunks of furry flesh.

The six dogs remaining hesitated, deterred by the swift demise of their leaders. They warily circled their prey, growling and snapping, searching for a weakness, any opening they could exploit. A large Doberman, overeager, crouched and sprang.

Rikki was ready. He dropped to his right knee, below the hurtling dog, and swung his katana with all of his considerable strength.

The Doberman yipped as it lost three of its legs.

A shepherd attempted to reach the man while he was down on one knee, but its throat was neatly cut open before it could sink its fangs in its intended victim, and it withdrew, gurgling and whining, blood pumping everywhere.

The last three dogs were reluctant to engage the man. The sight of their dead or dying comrades, many writhing in sheer agony and uttering pitiable cries, was too much for them. They broke and ran, heading for the hill to the east.

Rikki slowly straightened, his alert eyes scanning

his fallen foes for any capable of jumping him.

All of them were out of commission.

Lexine, a silent, stupefied witness to the fierce fight, shook her head in disbelief.

Rikki glanced at her. "Are you all right?" he asked.

"Never been better," Lexine responded in a daze.

Rikki walked toward one of the crippled dogs, intending to dispatch the lot of them and put them out of their misery.

A burst of gunfire erupted from the direction of the other side of the hill, followed by a peculiar noise from above.

Rikki looked up, startled.

A strange flying contraption was almost overhead, bearing to the west, powered by a spinning blade on its top and a smaller one located at its rear.

"A red copter!" Lex shouted. "Slave hunters!"

A what? Rikki looked at her, puzzled.

"Did you hear those shots?" Lex inquired nervously.

Rikki nodded. "Was it the . . . Red copter?"

Lexine's green eyes widened as she stared over Rikki's left shoulder. "No," she replied, pointing. "It was them!"

Rikki turned and was surprised to discover the crest of the hill crammed with bikers. Where had they come from? Why hadn't he heard them approach? The answer to both questions was self-evident: they had approached from the east while he was battling the dog pack, and he'd been so intent on dispatching the dogs he'd failed to note the bikers. Until now.

The one called Cardew was with them.

"We've got to get out of here!" Lex exclaimed, starting to climb onto one of the abandoned motorcycles.

The riders on the crest gunned their bikes and roared down toward the pair below.

Lex, straddling the cycle, was futilely striving to start the machine. "What the hell is the matter with this thing!" she fumed. "Why won't it kick over?"

Rikki ignored her rhetorical question and faced the bikers. He noticed all of them wore black-leather apparel and all were armed. Two women were in the lead. One was a tall brunette, the other a hefty blonde.

Lexine jumped from the useless cycle and ran to another of the bikes. "We've got to get out of here!" she repeated.

Rikki knew it was too late. Departure was out of the question. Already 20 bikers appeared, and more were rumbling over the hill every second.

The tall bunette motioned with her right arm and the bikers fanned out, some veering to the left, others to the right, surrounding the man in black and Lexine.

Lexine, finally realizing escape was impossible, crossed to Rikki's side, standing to his left, her survival knife at the ready. "Looks like we blew it, handsome!" she shouted to make herself heard over the thundering cycles. "Sorry!"

Over 40 bikers had encircled the pair. At a signal from the brunette all of the riders killed their engines.

Rikki studied the brunette, the apparent leader. She wore a leather jacket and pants. A pair of revolvers were strapped around her lean waist, and Rikki recognized the handguns as Llama Super Comanche V's. Her facial features were angular and hard, her mouth set in a tight frown. Pale blue eyes regarded him with calculating intent. Under her right eye, in a ragged line from the eye to the tip of her chin, was an old scar, as if one side of her face had once been torn apart.

"So, Lex," said the brunette in a mocking, strident tone, "who's your boyfriend?" She smirked at Rikki.

"Leave him out of this," Lex stated. "It's me you want, Terza."

The woman named Terza glared at Lexine. "I want you, all right, sweetheart. You'll pay for trying to desert us! And so will lover boy here!"

"Leave him go!" Lex urged.

"No can do," Terza said, shaking her head. She looked at the bodies of Pat and the other two women. "Cardew told me what he did. This bastard is going to pay!"

"Listen!" one of the other bikers yelled.

From the west, distinctly audible, came the harsh chatter of machine guns.

"Look!" Cardew pointed westward.

Rikki shifted his stance. The red copter was perhaps a mile off, swooping above the highway. He instantly perceived the reason for the machine-gun fire: that thing was attacking the SEAL, was going after his friends. He had to reach them! But how? He was completely hemmed in by a wall of motorcycles.

"Do you think they're after one of us?" Cardew queried.

"None of our people are out that far," Terza said. "They must be after somebody else."

"Should we go check?" Cardew asked her.

"No," Terza answered. "We're going to take these two back before that copter returns." She paused, absently biting her lower lip, reflecting. "Whoever the copter is after is doing us a favor. I was sure the Reds would strafe us after we shot at them. Our rifles and hanguns ain't much use against their firepower."

The portly blonde, a squat woman with a perpetually mean expression, nodded at Lexine. "Climb up behind me," she ordered.

"Get bent, Erika!" Lex retorted.

Terza raised her left arm and over two dozen firearms were trained on Rikki and Lexine. "What's it gonna be?" she asked Lex. "If you and lover boy don't mount up, right now, we'll blow you away!"

Rikki, despite his calm exterior, was in a profound turmoil. There was no way he could hope to prevail against so many opponents. If he resisted, they would simply kill him. But if he allowed them to take him into St. Louis, he would be unable to aid Blade and

Hickok. He scanned the rifles, revolvers, and pistols pointed in his direction and knew he had no choice. He would be of no benefit to his friends dead.

"Drop the sword!" Terza commanded.

Rikki reluctantly obeyed.

"And the knife!" Terza snapped at Lexine.

Lex angrily tossed her weapon aside.

"Now get behind Erika," Terza told Lexine.

The redhead glanced into Rikki's eyes for a moment, wanting to let him know how sorry she was to have involved him in this mess.

"Move it!" Terza barked.

Lexine mounted Erika's bike.

Terza grinned and winked at Rikki. "And you, lover boy, can get behind me."

Rikki dutifully slid his small frame behind the brunette. He stared at his bloody katana, averse to leaving it. His katana was an extension of himself, his most prized possession, a symbol of his Warrior nature, an essential component for a true samurai. Ordinarily, he would not relinquish the weapon under any circumstances. But this was an exception, and it just might save the lives of his companions.

Terza led the cyclists to the east.

As they crossed the low hill, Rikki caught his first glimpse of St. Louis. He saw many towering buildings miles off, the skyline of the inner city. What had they called those tremendous structures in the days before World War III, before the Big Blast—as the Family referred to the war? After a minute he remembered. Skyscrapers. He'd seen such buildings once before, in Denver, Colorado, and after his return to the Home had researched them in the Family library. Prewar architecture fascinated him, as it did a majority of the Family. Many of the photographic books contained stunning pictures of incredible buildings: edifices reaching into the heavens, bizarre spherical structures and glistening domes, individual residences of every shape and size—some too fantastic to comprehend. Rikki had received the impression each city was a veritable concrete and metal labyrinth. How could people have lived in such an unhealthy environment? Deprived of rejuvenating contact with the earth, denied the pleasure of experiencing the joys of nature, of strolling through a verdant forest pulsing with the vibrant rhythms of animal life? It was no wonder the cities reputedly festered with asocial, deviate, and criminal behavior. And here he was, heading into a sweltering city.

The cyclists passed a small group of six bikers, parked at the side of the road. Rikki spotted a small trailer hitched to one of the bikes. On the blue trailer was a cage, and in the cage were the three dogs from the pack. Two other trailers, both empty, were connected to stout bars to other cycles. So now he knew how the Leather Knights transported their hunting dogs.

Small buildings appeared on both sides of the highway. Frame homes, brick houses, and others, comprising the outskirts of St. Louis, the suburbs. Some were occupied, as evidenced by their well-preserved state, their clean sidings, intact windows, and neatly trimmed lawns. One man was cutting his grass with an ancient rotary mower. Other homes were obviously vacant, their windows broken, their roofs and porches sagging or collapsed. Some of the residents waved at the Leather Knights.

"The people seem to like you," Rikki commented in Terza's right ear.

Terza glanced over her right shoulder. "Why shouldn't they, lover boy? We keep the peace, don't we? We protect 'em from the lousy Reds. The streets are safe at night. Why shouldn't they like us?" she demanded indignantly.

Indeed. Why shouldn't they? Had he erred in siding with Lex against the others? Rikki looked to his left and found Lexine watching him. She grinned sheepishly and averted her eyes, her long tresses whipping in the wind as Erika's bike paced Terza's. The sight of Lexine's features was enough to confirm his decision; there was an air of truthful sincerity about the woman.

The Leather Knights continued into the inner city area. The further they went, the more indications of habitation they encountered. Bikers seemed to be everywhere, but there was a singular lack of other vehicles. No cars or trucks or jeeps.

Rikki searched for a landmark and tried to read every street sign they passed. Many of the signs were missing or illegible, the letters having faded with the passing of a century. The bikers made a number of turns, some to the east, some to the south, ever bearing inward, deeper into the grimy bowels of the metropolis.

A large sign appeared. From it, Rikki learned they were traveling east on Market Street. Huge buildings lined the south side of Market Street, while there was a park bordering the northern edge. Something ahead, something gleaming in the sunlight, arrested Rikki's attention. He couldn't see it clearly at first, but after a minute it became visible, rearing skyward to the east.

Rikki gawked, amazed. What was it? What purpose did it serve? The structure was gigantic, some sort of tremendous, glistening arc or arch. The bikers wheeled their cycles to the left, driving north on Broadway. As they turned, Rikki gazed to his right and saw a mysterious, gargantuan building, a circular affair. He caught only a glimpse of it out of the corner of his eye.

A city of marvels!

The street ahead became crowded with Leather Knights, most of them parked on the sidewalks and involved in idle conversations. They turned to stare as Terza's cavalcade rode past.

Where were they going?

A dingy edifice appeared to the left. Two faint but readable words were painted on one wall: Bus

Terminal. The street and lot to the south of the terminal were filled with Leather Knights. They gathered around as Terza angled her cycle up to a cracked curb and killed her motor. The other riders did the same.

"Who's the runt?" a bearded biker inquired.

"Lex is back!" shouted a woman.

Terza slid from her bike and motioned for Rikki to do likewise. "Gather round!" she yelled to the throng.

Rikki saw Erika yank Lex from her bike. Lexine clenched her fists in frustration, and Erika shoved her toward Rikki.

"We caught the traitor!" Terza announced. "Just like I said we would!"

"Where's Mira?" asked a husky woman.

"Wasted," Terza responded. "And she isn't the only one. This sucker," and she nodded at Rikki, "wasted three of our sisters!"

There was a detectable stir in the assembled Leather Knights as each and every one fixed a baleful glare on the man in black.

"We know what we do with traitors!" Terza bellowed. "And we know what to do to anyone who wastes one of our own!"

"Let Slither have 'em!" cried a furious woman.

"Slither!" echoed another woman.

Dozens of voices rose in unison, almost as if they were chanting. "Slither! Slither! Slither!"

"I demand a trial!" Lexine said to Terza.

Terza smirked. "Traitors don't deserve trials!" She stood aside, waving her left hand toward Rikki and Lexine.

The Leather Knights swarmed in, enclosing Rikki and Lexine in a sea of black leather and sweaty flesh. Hands brutally grabbed the duo and propelled them along the street.

Rikki mentally debated the wisdom of resisting. There was a possibility he might be able to fight his

CAPITAL RUN 39

way free of the mob, but he would have to leave Lexine behind to succeed and he would not abandon her under any circumstances. He noted her cool composure, her defiant demeanor, and admired her calculated courage. Here was a woman after his own heart!

The Leather Knights pulled, pushed, and shoved their captives to the east, in the direction of a wide body of water.

Rikki recognized the river ahead. They were being led toward the Missouri River. Why? What connection did the river have with the one called Slither?

Terza, walking alongside the prisoners, followed Rikki's glance. "It's the Mississippi River," she told him.

"I know," Rikki replied.

"Are you in the mood for a bath?" Terza asked.

"Not really," Rikki said.

"Too bad, turkey!" Terza laughed. "You're gonna get one whether you like it or not!"

Rikki tried to see the scenery on either side of the street, to serve as a reference for later use, but the mass of bikers prevented him from accomplishing his aim.

The Leather Knights bore to the right, leaving the road and marching down to the river. Trees lined the bank. Below a spreading maple tree was an old wooden dock, dilapidated beyond hope of redemption. One of the maple's thick lower branches extended over the dock and the murky water beyond.

The crowd halted.

"I'm sorry I got you into this," Lex said to Rikki.

"Ahhh. How sweet!" Erika cuffed Lexine across the mouth. "You bitch!"

Two ropes were produced and a pair of leather-garbed women carried them to the end of the dock. With practiced ease they tossed each rope over the lower branch in the maple tree, then turned and leered at the prisoners.

"Get moving!" Terza ordered, and shoved Lexine.

Rikki walked along the dock, the wood swaying under his feet. He was surprised by the rampant stupidity the Leather Knights displayed. Why hadn't they thought to frisk him for additional weapons? Why hadn't they interrogated him? They were enraged by the deaths of their fellow Knights, but unrestrained emotion was a pitiful substitute for seasoned leadership and responsible judgment.

Lexine reached the two women at the end of the dock first. One of them secured her rope to Lexine's wrists, using one end of the rope for each arm. The woman gleefully tied the knots as tightly as she could.

The second woman hauled Rikki to her side and performed a similar binding operation on him.

Lexine was watching the surface of the water, her green eyes darting to the left and the right.

"What's down there?" Rikki queried her.

"Find out for yourself," said the woman who had tied him, and she grunted as she abruptly shoved him from the dock.

Rikki's arms were wrenched upward by the force of the rope tugging on his arms. He dropped a few feet before the rope brought him up short with a jarring snap. The pain was intense but fleeting. He grit his teeth and looked to his right.

Lexine was also dangling above the river. Her eyes were closed, her mouth twisted in agony.

Rikki appraised their situation. Both of them were about a yard from the dock, Rikki being slightly further away because his rope had been placed beyond Lexine's on the limb. His custom-made black shoes, constructed from dyed deer hide and cougar sinew, were only a foot above the Mississippi.

The Leather Knights gathered along the west bank, collectively surveying the expanse of water beyond the dock, eagerly waiting.

But for what?

4

The rocket was almost on them!

Blade instinctively executed the only maneuver possible; he wrenched the steering wheel to the right, causing the transport to lurch sideways, angling the passenger side of the vehicle, Hickok's side, away from the hurtling rocket.

With an ear-splitting roar the rocket struck the highway about seven feet in front of the SEAL. Massive chunks of asphalt, dirt, and rocks were blasted upward. A jolting concussion, an irresistible shock wave of puissant force, slammed broadside into the transport like an unstoppable tidal wave onto a beach. The synthetic body withstood the shattering explosion intact, but the SEAL was flipped onto its passenger side and propelled several feet along the highway before it came to a rest.

Inside the SEAL, the two Warriors were tossed and buffeted by the tumbling vehicle. Blade struggled to maintain his grip on the steering wheel to prevent himself from falling onto the gunman. Hickok crashed against the passenger door, the handle digging into his ribs. The provisions in the rear section spilled over the central seat. One box of ammunition flew forward and narrowly missed Blade's head.

Blade leaped into action as soon as the SEAL stopped moving. He lunged for the driver's door and threw it open. Using the steering wheel for support, he vaulted outside onto the upturned body.

The helicopter was still hovering to the east of the transport.

Hickok was trying to untangle his contorted form from the bottom of the SEAL. "Dangblasted varmints! I'll fix their wagon!"

"Stay put!" Blade ordered. "I'll try to lead them off." He jumped to the ground and ran toward the trees on the south side of the highway.

The helicopter, as if it were a metallic bird of prey, swooped down for the coup de grace.

Blade weaved as he ran, knowing the copter would open up again with its machine guns.

A crackling spray of lead from the whirlybird confirmed his expectation.

Blade flinched as the earth around him was stitched by a pattern of lethal slugs. He was only five feet from cover and safety when he risked a hasty glance over his left shoulder.

The helicopter wasn't more than ten feet above the SEAL, swiveling for a clearer shot at its intended victim.

Blade dodged to the left, and as he did his right foot caught in something and he went down, sprawling onto his hands and knees, vulnerable and helpless.

The helicopter pilot instantly took advantage of the situation by edging his copter nearer to the trees and his rising target.

Blade, only two feet from the trees, braced for the impact of the machine-gun bullets, realizing it would be impossible for the copter gunner to miss at such close range.

Gunshots boomed to the Warrior's rear, but they weren't the sound of .45-caliber machine guns; they were the welcome bang-bang-bang of a pair of pearl-handled Colt Python .357 Magnum revolvers.

Blade spun around.

The gunman was only partially visible, with his

shoulders and arms protruding from the open door on the driver's side of the SEAL.

What did Hickok hope to accomplish? Blade wondered. The Pythons against an armed helicopter were seemingly insurmountable odds. But then he saw the gunman's intent and grinned.

Hickok was going for the tail blade. The Colts bucked in his hands as he fired six shots in swift succession. He had to distract the copter gunner's attention from Blade, and he succeeded.

On the gunman's sixth shot, the helicopter suddenly lurched to one side, then began swerving back and forth. It darted upward, its flight uneven, the pilot evidently experiencing difficulty in keeping the craft level.

"Got ya'!" Hickok said, elated.

The helicopter continued to ascend until it was 100 feet above the highway. Its front end dipped as the craft proceeded to speed to the east. Within less than a minute the helicopter was a dark dot on the eastern horizon.

Blade walked to the transport. "Thanks," he said, smiling at Hickok. "You saved my life."

Hickok adopted the air of casual nonchalance. "It was a piece of cake," he declared, then smiled. "Besides, I didn't want your missus bawling her brains out on my buckskins."

Blade's brow furrowed as he studied the SEAL. "We have a major problem on our hands."

"When don't we?" Hickok said. He slid to the ground and immediately set about reloading his Pythons.

Blade slowly made an inspection of the transport, searching for structural damage. He conducted a complete circuit of the vehicle.

"What did you find, pard?" Hickok asked as Blade rounded the front end.

"It looks okay," Blade replied.

Hickok's left Colt was already in its holster. He ejected the last spent shell from his right Python, removed a bullet from his gunbelt, and dropped it into the cylinder. Satisfied, he swung the cylinder closed and twirled the Colt into his right holster.

"We won't really know how it is until we try to start it," Blade said, pondering their dilemma, "and we can't try starting it until we have it upright again."

Hickok frowned. "How the blazes are we gonna do that?"

"I wish I knew." Blade stared at the east. This mission, like all the others, had devolved into a typical fiasco. Why was it events never went as you planned? Why did things always have to go wrong? Here they were, not more than ten miles from their destination, and now their transport was inoperational and one of them was missing. What next?

"What are we gonna do about Rikki?" Hickok inquired.

Blade stroked his square chin. "There is no way we can right the SEAL on our own," he said, reasoning aloud. "We could do it if we had enough people or another vehicle and a lot of rope—"

"Which we don't have," Hickok interrupted.

"—so we'll have to go look for what we need," Blade stated. "And since we have to find Rikki, we'll kill two birds with one stone. One of us will head for St. Louis."

"One of us?" Hickok repeated.

"Just one of us," Blade confirmed.

"Why not both of us?" Hickok wanted to know.

"We can't leave the SEAL unprotected," Blade explained.

"We've done it before," Hickok protested. "All we have to do is lock this contraption up tight as a drum and it'll be safe and sound until we get back."

Blade pointed at the exposed undercarriage. "And what about that?"

"What about it?" Hickok asked, puzzled.

"The bottom of the SEAL might not be as impervious as the special body," Blade said. "Someone could come along and damage it, render it totally useless. I can't allow that to happen. The SEAL is invaluable to our Family. You know that."

Hickok looped his thumbs in his gunbelt near the buckle. "And which one of us gets to waltz into St. Louis?"

"I'm going," Blade said.

"Why can't I go?" Hickok demanded.

"Because I said so," Blade stated, settling the matter. Since he was the head of the Warriors, his decisions were final.

"What am I supposed to do while you're gone?" Hickok groused. "Twiddle my thumbs?"

"You can check our supplies," Blade instructed the pouting gunman. "Make sure they're okay and clean up the mess inside."

"What if something happens to you?" Hickok queried. "How long should I wait?"

Blade considered a moment. "Give me three days. I should find Rikki and be back by then."

"Fine," Hickok said. "Three days it is. But if you're not back here by then, I'm comin' after you, SEAL or no SEAL."

Blade chuckled. "Keep an eye peeled while I collect the provisions I'll need." So saying, he hoisted himself up and climbed into the transport. The interior of the vehicle was a mess, but he found the items he wanted without much difficulty: a canteen, a canvas backpack confiscated from soldiers in Wyoming, strips of venison jerky, extra magazines for his Commando, and the Commando itself. He stuffed the canteen, jerky, and magazines into the backpack and clambered to the open driver's door. "Here," he said to the gunman, and tossed the backpack.

Hickok caught it with a deft flick of his left wrist.

Blade used his powerful arms to haul his body from

the SEAL. Holding the Commando in his left hand, he leaped to the highway.

"You sure ain't takin' much, pard," Hickok observed, hefting the light backpack.

"I won't be gone that long," Blade said. He took the backpack and handed the Commando to the gunman.

"I hope Rikki is okay," Hickok remarked, gazing eastward.

"Rikki can take care of himself," Blade commented. He placed his brawny arms through the backpack straps. "You make certain that you stay out of trouble while I'm gone."

"Who? Me?" Hickok quipped. He gave the Commando to the Alpha Triad leader. "You're the one who'd best take care."

"May the Spirit watch over you," Blade said. He started walking due east. About 50 yards ahead was a turn in the road, the highway evidently bearing slightly to the southeast. Blade could feel the heat from the sun on his broad back and legs as he marched along. He stopped when he reached the turn and glanced at the SEAL. Hickok was still standing exactly where he had left him, the gunman's thumbs hooked in his gunbelt. Blade couldn't discern Hickok's face clearly, but he received the impression the gunman was frowning. Blade knew Hickok didn't like the idea of staying behind one bit, but the gunman was too loyal a Warrior to lodge more than a minor protest.

Blade waved.

Hickok began jumping up and down and flapping his arms like crazy. After a minute he ceased and made a show of blowing a farewell kiss in Blade's direction.

Blade shook his head as the gunman started laughing. Thank the Spirit the gunman was on this mission! Rikki was naturally rather taciturn, and the lengthy ride would have been monotonous without the loquacious gunfighter. Blade resumed his journey, following the highway, sticking to the middle of the road. If anything came at him, he'd have the time to see it coming and respond accordingly. He raked his eyes across the forest to the right and left of the crumbling asphalt, alert for any sign of a mutate or other horror.

Time passed.

Blade was less than a mile from the SEAL when he spied the corpses on the road ahead. And three—what were they?—motorcyles!

What was this?

He slowed, advancing cautiously, his finger on the trigger of the Commando.

Bodies. Lots and lots of bodies.

Was Rikki's one of them?

Blade paused 15 feet from the prone forms. He could see 3 dead women and counted 13 dogs, a few of which were alive, whining and whimpering in torment.

What had happened? Had the helicopter done this?

Blade walked up to the first corpse and examined the area. Why would anyone leave three motorcycles, apparently functional, out here in the middle of nowhere? Could he ride one? he wondered. If he could manage to figure out how it was done, he'd find Rikki that much faster. He'd never ridden one before, but that didn't—

No!

Blade froze as his gaze rested on a bloody sword lying amidst the slain canines. It was a katana! Rikki's katana! Blade would recognize the sword anywhere! And there was the scabbard! But Rikki would never cast aside his cherished weapon. Or would he? There was no sign of Rikki's body, and it was doubtful anyone would bother to cart it off but leave the three women behind. So Rikki must be alive, and he must have deliberately left the kantana as a warning to his fellow Warriors. The katana's presence conclusively proved Rikki *had* been here, but was gone now.

To where?

St. Louis?

Blade retrieved the sword and the scabbard. He wiped the blade clean on a dead dog and slid the katana into its scabbard.

A low rumbling sounded from beyond a hill to the east.

Blade quickly eased the scabbard under his belt, aligning it in front of the Bowie knife on his left hip. He crouched and darted across the road and into the trees on the right side of the highway. He was barely out of sight before more motorcycles appeared at the top of the hill. Without hesitating, they descended toward the bodies.

Would Rikki be with them?

Blade peered around the trunk of an oak tree, watching the approaching riders.

There were three motorcycles, each hauling a trailer with a cage on top. In one of the cages were three dogs. Two men were on each motorcycle: the driver and a passenger, each man straddling his narrow seat with accomplished ease, despite the numerous ruts and bumps the bikes struck as they sped nearer.

They reminded Blade of the Cavalry, the superb horsemen occupying the Dakota territory. These bikers displayed the same casual mastery of their cycles shown by the Cavalry toward their horses. Whether it was man and machine or man and faithful steed, both seemed as one.

What was going on?

The three cycles braked and halted near the bodies. One after the other the drivers shut off their motors.

One of the passengers, a skinny man with baggy leather pants and a bushy brown beard, sighed as he eased to the ground. "I don't see why we had to be the ones," he said bitterly. "She could have sent somebody else."

"Oh, yeah?" countered one of the drivers. "Who? We were the closest."

CAPITAL RUN 49

"Besides," added another, "I think Terza was pissed at us over what happened to the dogs."

The bearded biker stared at the dogs littering the highway. "It wasn't our fault," he said sadly.

"It was that damn guy in black," commented another.

Guy in black? That had to be Rikki! Blade inched a bit further around the tree, not wanting to miss a word.

"Who was that joker?" asked a portly biker as he climbed from his cycle.

"Beats me," answered the bearded one. "The messenger from Terza didn't know. He told me she wanted us to get these bikes and take care of the dogs. That was all."

"Damn!" fumed the third driver as he walked up to the slain dogs. "Look at this! How the hell did the guy do it?"

The bearded biker shook his head. "I don't know. But he must be one mean son of a bitch."

One of the other men snorted. "Not for long, he won't be. You can bet Terza will rack his ass for what he did to Pat and the others."

"And we'll probably miss out on the fun," complained the third driver.

"I wouldn't say that," interjected a deep voice from the edge of the highway.

Startled, the bikers spun, shocked to behold a towering man with dark hair and simmering eyes pointing a machine gun in their general direction.

"Who the hell are you?" demanded the bearded biker.

"Would you believe the tooth fairy?" replied the big man.

The bikers exchanged confused, worried glances.

"Drop your weapons," Blade commanded.

All of the bikers were armed, four with revolvers and two with knives. A Winchester was strapped to one of their motorcycles.

Blade waited, sensing one of them would make a play, watching their eyes for the telltale hint of an impending violent attack. Very few fighters could disguise this instinctive reaction, a slight tightening of the eyes, a shifting of the pupils, prior to galvanizing their body into action. Almost every fighter telegraphed his assault in one way or another, whether it was a movement of the eyes or a contracting of the shoulder muscles right before he threw a punch. Only an extremely skilled and accomplished fighter was capable of perfectly masking his intent. Such a fighter didn't reveal his maneuver or foreshadow his blow beforehand; he simply executed it with lightning speed and devastating results. While all the Family's Warriors were trained in hand-to-hand combat, only a few demonstrated this exceptional ability of concealment, and Blade knew of only one who was the acme of perfection: Rikki-Tikki-Tavi.

One of the bikers, a hefty, unkempt individual with pink hair and an earring in his left lobe, was cautiously moving his right hand toward the revolver tucked under his belt.

"I don't want to kill you if I don't have to," Blade said, hoping they would wisely avoid a clash.

They weren't that wise.

Pink Hair clutched at his revolver, and that was the signal for the rest of them to go for their respective weapons.

Blade was left with no other option. He swung the Commando in an arc as he pulled the trigger, holding the barrel at chest height.

Pink Hair was the first to drop, his torso racked by the Commando's heavy slugs, his body spurting crimson geysers as he was flung backwards onto the highway. The three other bikers with guns were likewise decimated. One of the bikers with a knife managed to whip his weapon from its sheath and lunge at the giant with the machine gun, but a veritable hail of lead knocked him for a loop. Only one biker was left standing, untouched, with his knife partially drawn; it was the skinny man with the baggy leather pants and the bushy brown beard.

"Drop it or die!" Blade snapped.

Bushy Beard promptly discarded his knife. "Don't k-kill me, m-mister!" he wailed, stuttering, in fear for his life.

Blade strolled up to the biker. "Whether you die or not will depend on you. I'm going to ask some questions and I want truthful answers." He rammed the Commando barrel into the biker's abdomen. "One answer I don't like and you're going to develop a split personality. Understand?"

The biker nodded vigorously.

"What's your name?" Blade asked.

"Jeff," the biker replied.

"What are you?"

Jeff's eyes narrowed and his brow furrowed, as if he was puzzled. "How do you mean?"

"Are you part of a gang?" Blade queried. He nodded at the bodies around him. "All of you wear black leather. Why?"

"That's our color, man," Jeff said.

"Color?"

"Yeah. Where are you from? Don't they have colors where you come from?" Jeff inquired.

Blade pressed on the Commando and Jeff blanched. "I'll ask the questions," Blade reminded him.

"Sure thing," Jeff promptly responded.

"What is the name of your gang?"

"We're called the Leather Knights," Jeff said proudly.

"And do the Leather Knights have their . . ." Blade paused, trying to recall the words he wanted. Once before, during Alpha Triad's run to the Twin Cities, he had dealt with street gangs. What was the name they used for their territory? Something to do with grass or sod or—" . . . turf in St. Louis?" he said as the word came to him.

"St Louis is our turf," Jeff boasted.

"The Leather Knights control the entire city?" Blade interrogated the biker.

"Yep." Jeff beamed. "Have for years."

"Detail the history of the Leather Knights," Blade instructed.

"What?" Jeff almost laughed. "Are you kidding?"

Blade leaned forward, his raging eyes burning into Jeff's. "Do I look like I'm kidding?"

Jeff gulped. "No, sir. You sure don't."

"Then start talking."

"There's not much to tell," Jeff said in a frightened tone. "I don't know a lot about it, honest!"

"You must know something."

"All I know is what I've heard," Jeff explained, "what some of the old-timers have told me."

"I'm waiting."

Jeff reflected a moment. "The Leather Knights got started way back before the war," he detailed. "When the war broke out, most of the people in St. Louis took off. I think they were evacuated by the Government, or something like that. Anyway, the Knights stayed put and got involved in some fights with two or three other gangs over who was going to claim the turf. The Knights came out on top."

"Are there any other people in St. Louis besides the Leather Knights?" Blade asked.

"Yep. Bunches. A lot of people strayed back after the war was over. I don't know how many there are now, but there's got to be at least a couple of thousand," Jeff said.

"How many Leather Knights are there?" Blade questioned him.

"Six hundred, if you count the studs," Jeff answered.

"Studs?"

"Yeah. I'm a stud. The guys you just wasted were studs. You'd be a stud, too, if you were a Knight."

Now it was Blade's turn to be confused. "I don't understand," he admitted.

"You've got balls, don't you?"

"Balls?"

"Nuts. Coconuts, man. Gonads," Jeff said, accenting the last word.

Blade was more bewildered than before. "What do my sexual organs have to do with it?"

"Everything. If you ain't got nuts and a pecker, you can't hardly be a stud," Jeff explained.

Blade's eyes widened in comprehension. "You mean all of the men are studs?"

Jeff snickered. "The foxes ain't got the hardware, if you get my drift."

"And the studs control the Leather Knights?" Blade speculated.

Jeff snorted again. "Where'd you ever get a dumb idea like that?" He hesitated, appalled at his own stupidity. "I didn't mean anything by that crack," he quickly blurted out. "Honest!"

"If the men . . . the studs . . . don't control the Leather Knights, then who does?" Blade demanded.

"Who else? The foxes."

"The women?"

"Why do you look so surprised? Ain't it the same where you come from?" Jeff inquired.

Blade shook his head. "Our men and women share responsibility. You can't really say one dominates the other."

"You're putting me on!"

"I'm serious," Blade stated. "How did the women assume control of the Leather Knights?"

"It's always been that way," Jeff replied.

"Always?"

Jeff frowned. "I did hear a story once, but I thought the old guy who told me was wacko. He said that long ago, way back about the time of the war, the men ran the show. But all the fighting over our turf killed off most of the men. The Leather Knights became top dog in St. Louis, but few of the men survived. So the foxes, the mamas, sort of took over."

"And the women have been running the show ever since," Blade concluded.

"They do now," Jeff affirmed.

"How many of the Knights are studs?"

"Oh, about two hundred," Jeff answered.

"But you said there are six hundred Knights?"

"That's right," Jeff said.

"And the other four hundred are all women?" Blade asked.

"Yep."

"That doesn't make sense," Blade said. "How can you have so many women and so few men?"

"We've got more men," Jeff responded. "Lots more. But the women don't let every man into the Leather Knights. Only enough to handle their dirty work."

"Dirty work?"

"Yeah. Things like the cleaning and the laundry and stuff like that. It's a real drag! I wouldn't of joined up, but it was the only way I could get me a bike," Jeff elaborated.

"Only the Knights are entitled to motorcycles?"

"Of course."

Blade stepped back, studying the biker, debating. He believed the man. But where did it leave him? What good did the knowledge do? In the final analysis, what did it matter whether the women or the men ran the Leather Knights and controlled St. Louis? Either way, getting Rikki out of there promised to be no easy task. "You mentioned a guy in black earlier."

"The one who wasted our dogs," Jeff said. "We were after Lex and Mira, when Cardew came hauling ass and told Terza about this guy in black who racked three sisters. That's what the women all call themselves. The sisters. Anyhow, Terza got real ticked off and ordered us to send the dogs out." Jeff paused. "I've been on the dog detail for six months. I'm so damn sick of dog shit I could scream."

"Back up a bit," Blade directed him. "Who are Lex and Mira? And Cardew and Terza?"

"Lex is one of the sisters," Jeff said. "She got tired of the Knights and was trying to split. But the sisters ain't allowed to split once they take the oath. As for Mira," he said, shifting to his right and pointing at a woman lying among the dogs, "she got racked."

"And Cardew and Terza?"

"Cardew is one of the studs. He was riding point when they caught up with Lex and Mira. He's the one who told us about the man in black."

"That leaves Terza," Blade reminded him.

"Terza is our head, man," Jeff revealed. "She runs the whole show."

"Terza rules the Leather Knights?"

"You got it."

"What kind of a woman is she?" Blade asked.

"She's one mean mother!" Jeff said. "She don't take any crap from anybody. Sort of like you."

Blade grinned. "Where are they holding the man in black?"

"Is he a friend of yours?"

"Yes. Where is he?"

"I don't know," Jeff answered.

Blade took a step forward.

"Hey!" Jeff held up his hands. "Really, man! I don't know where they've got him! He's in St. Louis, but that's all I know."

"What will they do? Hold him prisoner?" Blade inquired.

"The Leather Knights don't take no prisoners," Jeff said. "He may be dead by now. Terza don't like it when one of the sisters gets wasted, and your friend racked three. One of them, that one there," and he pointed at another corpse, "was called Pat, a real good buddy of Terza's. I imagine Terza will rack your friend first thing. Maybe take him out herself, or stake him out for Grotto, or even feed him to Slither."

Blade wanted to pose additonal questions, but he realized time was of the essence. He had to reach Rikki as swiftly as feasible. "You're taking me to St. Louis," he announced.

"You're crazy!" Jeff responded.

Blade hefted the Commando. "Pick a cycle. I'll ride behind you. Don't try anything funny," he warned.

Jeff glanced at the Bowies and the sword. "I'll take you, but there's no way you're gonna get your friend out in one piece."

"You let me worry about that. Start a bike." Blade waited while Jeff climbed on one of the cycles and kicked it over. He straddled the seat behind the Leather Knight and tapped Jeff's head with the Commando barrel. "Let's go."

Jeff gunned the bike, executed a U-turn, and headed toward the east. "This just isn't my day," he muttered to himself.

5

An hour must have elapsed, possibly longer.

Rikki's arms were aching, hurting from the sustained strain of being suspended from the coarse rope. Periodically he glanced at Lex, and although she never complained or uttered a moan or other sound it was obvious that she was in extreme agony.

The crowd on the bank had grown until over 200 men and women were now gathered for the event.

But what were they waiting for? Rikki scanned the river for the umpteenth time. What was down there? He had asked Lex once, but all she said in reply was "Slither." What was this Slither? It must be some sort of creature lurking in the river's depths. Rikki twisted and gazed at the watchers on the west bank. None of them was anywhere near the dock, which was good. But firearms were in abundant evidence, which was bad. How could he free himself and Lex and escape before Slither arrived and avoid being shot? "When will Slither show up?" he asked Lexine.

She shook her head, gritting her teeth as a spasm lanced her shoulders. "Any time," she said after the pain subsided. "It comes when it feels like it, when it's hungry."

"Is it a large animal? Reptile, amphibian, mammal, what?" Rikki inquired.

"I don't know," Lex said softly. "It's not like any other animal I know."

"A mutant," Rikki stated. Ever since the war a

century before, since the environment had been ravaged by massive dosages of radiation and deadly chemicals and other toxins, the animal life had altered drastically. The genetic constitution of many forms of wildlife had been radically affected by the radiation and chemicals; mutations had become commonplace. Bizarre carnivorous strains had developed. Giantism had appeared in some species. Although in some areas, such as the inhabited major cities still standing and in the Civilized Zone, the mutants had been ruthlessly exterminated over the years, there wasn't a solitary place on the continent completely safe from the biological deviates. Or so it was believed. One could crop up anywhere, anytime.

Like now.

There was a rustling and murmuring along the west bank.

Rikki glanced at the assembled mob, noting they were all staring upriver, to the north. He looked in the same direction and spotted a commotion in the water approximately 50 yards away.

"It's Slither!" Lex cried.

Nothing was visible on the surface of the Mississippi except for an eight-foot wake, a rippling of tiny waves expanding outward as a massive form swam under the water.

"Rikki . . ." Lex said.

Rikki faced her.

"I'm sorry. So sorry. I wanted to get to know you better," Lex told him sadly.

"We're not dead yet," Rikki reminded her.

Lex looked at the approaching monster. "Not yet," she said halfheartedly.

"And I'm not quite ready for the higher mansions," Rikki wryly declared. "So brace yourself."

"For what?"

"For this," Rikki said. As surreptitiously as possible, he had been striving to extricate his wrists from the ropes. After an hour of strenuous effort, constantly working his wrists back and forth, back and forth, while pulling downward at the same time, he had succeeded in loosening his right wrist. His arm wasn't free yet, but the coil of rope around his slim wrist had developed sufficient slack to enable him to escape. His exertion had torn the skin on both his wrists, and there was a crimson coating between the surface of his wrist and the rope. With the sweat from the heat and his prolonged effort, all it would take was one mighty tug and his right wrist would be free, one wrench at the right moment.

That moment was now.

The wake generated by the underwater creature was 40 yards off and closing.

The Leather Knights and others on the west bank were concentrating on the wake.

Rikki bunched his sinewy shoulder muscles and strained, adding his considerable strength to his body weight and the force of gravity. His right wrist slipped clear of the rope, leaving him dangling by his left arm. Instantly, his lean frame coiled into action. He swung his leg outward, forcing the rope to move, to carry his body out over the water. Even as the swinging motion began, his right hand reached behind his back to the brown pouch in the small of his back, the pouch containing his shuriken and other items. One of those items was his personalized kyoketsu-shogei, a double-edged five-inch knife attached to a lengthy, leather cord. At the other end of the cord was a metal ring. When still a child of ten, Rikki had become an expert with the weapon. The kyoketsu-shogei could be used in several ways: the knife alone could be wielded offensively or defensively; or, while he held the knife, the cord could be whipped around an opponent's arms or legs, rendering the enemy vulnerable to a slash from the knife; or the ring could be held in one hand and the cord whirled until the precise angle and trajectory were attained and with a flick of the wrist, a straightening of the arm, the knife flashed into an adversary's body.

The wake was 30 yards from the dock.

Rikki's sensitive fingers found the kyoketsu-shogei just as he attained the apex of his swing. He whisked it from the pouch, and as he began to sweep downward toward Lexine he slid the two-inch metal ring over his index finger while retaining a precarious grip on the knife with his thumb.

Someone on the west bank spotted the man in black's maneuver and gave a shout. "Look! What's he doing?"

The creature was only 20 yards from the dock, and a large, green hump had appeared at the center of the spreading wake.

Rikki tensed as he swung toward Lexine. The next several seconds were critical. If anyone on the west bank thought to open fire, Lex and he would be riddled before he could complete what he had in mind.

The huge thing in the Mississippi River had increased its speed, as if it sensed its prey was making a determined bid for freedom.

Lexine's green eyes widened in wonder as Rikki closed on her.

Rikki opened his legs and swiveled slightly to the left, wrapping his legs around Lexine's waist, the impact of his form against hers driving them inward, toward the bank and well clear of the dock.

The creature known as Slither was ten yards from the dock.

Rikki reached up, slashing at Lexine's rope with his knife. He freed her right wrist in one quick slash, but only partially succeeded in severing the rope on the left wrist before the people clustered on the bank went absolutely wild, cheering and screaming encouragement to the thing in the river.

Rikki glanced over his right shoulder.

A ten-foot-long serpentine neck had emerged from the murky depths. The face of the mutant was hideous, repulsive beyond belief. Two horny appendages protruded from the head, one on each side. The shape of the head was circular, with a sloping forehead and a slender, bony jaw. Its eyes were smoldering pools of ferocity. A hissing sound filled the humid air as the creature opened its wide mouth, displaying neat rows of tapered teeth. The face also had a bumpy or lumpy appearance, lending a hellish aspect to the monstrosity. The perpetually ravenous abomination closed on its targets with astonishing speed for something so gigantic.

Rikki sliced at the rope securing Lexine's left wrist again, and this time he was successful. Lexine sagged as the rope parted, and Rikki clamped his legs around her to prevent her from falling into the river. The toll on his own left arm was terrible; her added weight made it seem as if his arm would be torn from its socket. Undaunted by the torment, he looked at the creature.

Slither was almost upon them, the head not more than seven feet away and closing.

Now!

Rikki released Lexine, spreading his legs wide and dropping her into the Mississippi.

Slither, focused on the suspended man, ignored the plummeting woman.

Rikki, expecting to feel those razor fangs imbedded in his back any second, reached up and cut the rope holding his left arm. As he fell, he turned, knowing Slither had to be but inches from him.

It was. The creature was poised with open mouth, about to lunge and bite.

Rikki's feet were entering the river as he drove his right arm up and in, plunging the knife into Slither's left eye. Hot, fetid breath was on his face as the knife sank home to the hilt, and he released the ring as his body sank beneath the water. He bent at the waist and swam toward the bank, away from the mutant, heading downstream, to the south.

Something was breaking the surface of the water ahead of him. He glanced up and distinguished the outline of Lex's body. She was treading water, apparently searching for him.

There was a tremendous commotion in the river to his rear.

Rikki swam upward and reached Lexine, emerging a foot to her right.

"Thank God!" Lex exclaimed.

Rikki gulped in fresh air and gazed back at the dock.

Slither was in a blind rage, thrashing and convulsing, splashing water in every direction and driving mini-waves onto the west bank. Transfixed by the sight, the people on the bank were gaping at its death throes in amazement.

"We've got to keep moving," Rikki said to Lex. "They'll recover in a bit and be looking for us."

Lexine reached over and tenderly stroked his left cheek. "That's twice I owe you for saving my life."

"You'd do the same for me," Rikki stated, and began swimming southward.

Lexine paced him to his right, between him and the bank.

About 40 yards south of the dock, cloaking the west bank, was a thick stand of brush and trees.

"There!" Rikki said, pointing. "Hurry!"

They swam for all they were worth, and Rikki found himself admiring her endurance and ability. Not once during Slither's attack had she screamed or otherwise betrayed any hint of panic. The woman was brave, there was no doubt about that. And as a dedicated Warrior, Rikki appreciated courage the most.

Loud voices swelled from the vicinity of the dock.

Rikki and Lexine were only ten yards from the bank when a shot rang out, followed by another and another.

The water to Rikki's left was smacked by a slug, spraying water in his eyes.

Lexine reached the bank first and slid under the overhanging growth of a large bush.

Rikki joined her.

"Which way?" she asked.

Rikki continued swimming, hugging the bank. After 20 feet he spied a narrow strip of barren earth and swam toward it.

The shooting had ceased.

"They'll be after us," Lex predicted.

"I know," Rikki agreed. He climbed from the Mississippi and assisted Lex in joining him on the bank.

"What now?" Lex asked.

"Stay close," Rikki advised. He hurried to the south, hugging the river bank, sticking to the thickest undergrowth despite the difficulty in negotiating passage. Sharp thorns tore at their limbs and ripped their clothing. Pointed branches gouged them mercilessly when they weren't careful. The ground underfoot was often damp and slick. Flies and mosquitoes were everywhere, buzzing about their ears and alighting on any exposed skin. The mosquitoes, in particular, descended on them in bloodthirsty droves.

Clamorous voices could be heard well to their rear.

A stand of trees loomed ahead, and beyond the trees a field.

Rikki stopped behind one of the tall maples and peered around the trunk.

On the far side of the field was an enormous, ramshackle building.

"Do you know what that is?" Rikki asked.

Lex stood to his left. "An old warehouse, I think. Nobody uses it anymore."

"Let's go." Rikki ran across the field, dodging rocks and rusted pieces of discarded junk, Lexine on his heels.

The warehouse ran the length of two city blocks. All of the windows were broken or missing. Dust and dirt caked the exterior. A large opening beckoned on the northern side. A shattered door hung by its top hinge to the right of the opening.

Rikki darted into the dim interior and crouched to the right of the doorway, waiting for his eyes to adjust to the gloom.

Lex did likewise to the left of the door.

The floor was covered with broken crates and crumpled boxes of all shapes and sizes. Evidently, years ago, the warehouse had been systematically looted. At the west end of the structure was a glimmer of light.

Another doorway? Rikki stood and nodded, then took off, cautiously advancing between the crates and boxes and circumventing any debris in his path.

There was a faint scratching sound to their left.

"Did you hear that?" Lex asked.

Rikki nodded. He kept going, his ears alert for additional noises.

An audible patter of padded feet came from behind a wall of crates to their left.

"Something's pacing us," Lex said, stating the obvious.

Rikki hastened toward the western doorway. If it was an animal, then the light might discourage it.

The pit-pat of the mysterious feet increased their tempo.

Rikki reached behind his back and into his brown pouch. His fingers closed on empty space.

No!

Rikki's fingers probed the bottom of the pouch to be sure. It was definitely empty. But how? The answer came to him in a rush. He had neglected to properly close the pouch after removing the kyoketsu-shogei!

Undoubtedly, sometime during his swing on the rope, his plunge into the river, or his swim to the bank, the contents of his pouch had spilled out.

The stealthy pad of the feet was now coming from the top of the wall of crates.

Rikki scanned the cement floor for a possible weapon. He spotted a smashed crate on the floor ahead and ran to the pile of splintered wood. One spear-like piece drew his attention. He knelt and picked it up. About four feet long and the width of his wrist, it was flat on one end but tapered on the other.

"Rikki!" Lex shouted suddenly.

Rikki rose and spun.

A hairy visage was studying them from atop the crate wall. An extended black snout, capped with whiskers several inches long, was quivering as it sought their scent. Fiery reddish eyes fixed on them with baleful intent.

"It's a river rat," Lex said.

Rikki held his makeshift spear in his right hand. He'd been told about the rats in Thief River Falls and the Twin Cities, rats encountered by Blade, Hickok, and Geronimo. But he'd never seen them himself, and he'd never expected them to be this large. The head of the one on the crate wall was at least 12 inches in length. "Make for the west door," Rikki instructed her.

Lexine slowly edged past him and started running.

Rikki, his gaze on the rat, followed.

The river rat disappeared.

Rikki tensed. Where had the rodent gone? To summon others?

Lexine was ten feet ahead, weaving between the boxes and crates littering the aisle.

Something scraped to Rikki's left, and the slight sound saved his life.

Rikki whirled.

The rat was already in motion, leaping from the top of the wall of crates, its body as big and solid as a

Doberman's, its pronounced yellow incisors exposed as it snarled and hurtled downward.

"Rikki!" Lexine screamed.

Rikki angled his spear, the tapered tip elevated in his left hand, the flat end held in his right.

The river rat crashed toward its prey, its bulky body carrying it onto the point of the spear, the shaft tearing into its neck at the base of its hairy throat and exiting at the top of the head just behind the ears.

Rikki was slammed to the cement by the stunning impact. He ducked his head to one side as the rat's nasty teeth snapped at his eyes. His arms bulged as he struggled to retain his hold on the spear.

The rat was squealing and jerking back and forth, attempting to wrench free of the shaft.

A raking paw narrowly missed Rikki's face.

And then Lex was there, standing behind the rat, a heavy metal pipe in her hands, and she crashed her club onto the rat's skull. Once. Twice. Three times.

The rat abruptly gurgled and stiffened, vomit bursting from its vile mouth.

Rikki kicked clear of the rat and rolled to his right, his own stomach inadvertently heaving as the rat's vomit spattered onto his chest. He jumped to his feet, forcing his stomach to subside, his nose assailed by the nauseating stench of the rat's puke.

The front of his black shirt was liberally sprinkled with the disgorged matter.

Rikki quickly stripped the shirt from his chest and flung it to the floor.

"Rikki!"

Rikki glanced up at Lexine's warning.

Two more rats were perched on the crate wall.

"The west door!" Rikki yelled.

Lex took off.

Rikki raced on her heels, watching the rats over his left shoulder.

One of the rats vanished, but the other bounded along the top of the crates, pursuing the humans.

CAPITAL RUN

The west doorway was visible now, not more than 15 yards distant.

Rikki was beginning to think they would reach the doorway without further trouble, but he was wrong.

Lexine unexpectedly stopped, holding her club in front of her.

A rat was on the floor ahead, blocking their path to the door.

Rikki reached Lex.

The second rat was still on top of the crate wall.

Rikki grabbed the metal pipe from Lexine. "When I make my move," he said, "go for the door."

"I won't leave you," Lex declared.

"You must leave—" Rikki began.

The river rat on top of the crates abruptly screeched and launched itself into the air.

The rat blocking the exit tittered and charged.

They were working in unison!

Rikki shoved Lexine to one side. He glanced up, bracing himself, as the rat from the crates dived downward. The second rat was ten feet off, squealing as it surged forward. He clenched the heavy pipe, relying on his superb reflexes, knowing one misstep would prove fatal.

The rat from the crates reached the Warrior first.

Rikki's body was a blur as he swung the pipe and twisted aside, his blow smacking onto the rat's head, and he was already turning to confront the second rat, the pipe arching around and up and catching the second rat on the tip of its twitching nose.

There was a resounding racket as the rat from the crates struck a pile of boxes and tumbled to the hard floor, while the second rat was jarred backward by the force of Rikki's blow. It retreated several steps, shaking its head, stunned.

"Stay close!" Rikki cried, and ran toward the rat still blocking the west door.

The rat skittered to the left, snapping at the pipe as Rikki aimed another blow at its face.

Rikki swung three times, each time missing as the odious rodent skipped out of range, but he succeeded in driving the rat away from the aisle, clearing the path to the doorway.

The rat from the crate wall had recovered and was cautiously stalking them.

Lexine was searching for anything she could utilize as a weapon.

Rikki grabbed her right hand. Keeping his eyes on the rat from the wall and constantly waving the metal pipe at the other rat, he began backing toward the doorway.

Neither rodent showed any inclination to pursue them too closely.

Rikki and Lex hastily withdrew, their backs to the doorway, watching the rats.

"They don't like the light," Lex commented.

Rikki was relieved when they finally emerged from the dim warehouse. The brilliant light of the scorching sun temporarily dazzled them as they turned away from the warehouse.

"Going somewhere?" a female voice asked.

In the instant his vision cleared, Rikki perceived their predicament.

"No!" Lex exclaimed.

Terza, the blonde named Erika, Cardew, and 25 other Leather Knights were standing not eight feet away, ringing the west door, all of them pointing guns at the man in black and the redhead.

"Having fun?" Erika cracked sarcastically, her jowly jaw trembling as she snickered at the pair.

"We heard your yelling over by the trees and came to investigate," Terza said coldly. "Did the rats give you a hard time?"

Rikki didn't answer.

"So what now?" Lex demanded.

"What do you think?" Terza angrily retorted. She looked at Rikki and grinned. "You're one tough son of a bitch, you know that, dude? You've wasted three of our sisters, butchered our dogs, and even managed to escape from Slither. And now this! Now you get away from the rats! You're incredible, bastard!"

Rikki's features were like granite.

"I've decided I shouldn't be in such a rush to kill you off," Terza said.

"Should we thank you now or later?" Lex asked.

Terza glanced at Lexine. "Not you, sweetheart. I was talking to lover boy here. We can waste you anytime."

Cardew took a step toward the duo, his Browning Auto Pistol in his right hand. "Let me do it, Terza!"

Rikki moved in front of Lexine.

Terza's blue eyes narrowed. "What have we here? Don't tell me lover boy really cares about you, Lex?"

Lex didn't answer.

"Ain't this interesting," Terza remarked thoughtfully.

"Can I blow her away now?" Cardew inquired hopefully.

"No, dipshit," Terza replied. "I've got a better idea."

"Like what?" Erika queried.

"You'll see soon enough," Terza said. She nodded at Rikki. "Drop the pipe."

Rikki hesitated.

"Drop the pipe or I let Cardew blow Lex away," Terza warned him.

Rikki dropped the pipe.

Terza started laughing.

"What's so funny?" Erika asked.

"I've got 'em right where I want 'em," Terza said.

"What do you mean?" Erika inquired, perplexed.

"You'll see," Terza promised. She faced Cardew. "Listen up, airhead! Erika and I are going to split. I want you to bring those two to the library—"

"You mean the book place?" Cardew interrupted.

Terza sighed. "Yeah, mush-for-brains! The book place. Hold 'em there until I arrive."

"Will do," Cardew said.

"And Cardew," Terza added.

"Yes?"

"If they get away from you I'll have your balls hacked off and force you to eat 'em. Got it?"

Cardew swallowed hard. "I got it," he guaranteed.

"That's a good boy," Terza said. She winked at Erika and they walked off to the north across the field.

"Okay, asshole!" Cardew snapped, stepping up to Rikki and gripping his right arm. "Let's get in gear!"

Rikki hardly seemed to move other than a rippling roll of his right shoulder, but Cardew lost his hold and stumbled backward two yards before he could recover his footing.

"Damn you!" Cardew waved his Browning at Rikki. "One more fancy move out of you—"

"And what?" Lex interjected. "Terza said you're to take us to the library. You can't kill us."

"Maybe I can't kill you," Cardew said, leering maliciously at her, "but there's nothing to stop me from roughing you up a bit. Terza didn't say I had to get you there in one piece."

Lex glared at Cardew.

"So what's it gonna be, buster?" Cardew asked Rikki. "We can do this the easy way or the hard way. It's up to you."

Rikki stared at Lex for a moment, his expression unreadable. Finally he turned to Cardew. "I will not resist the trip to the library," he said.

"You're not as dumb as you look," Cardew quipped. He waved at a tall black biker and a burly one with Hispanic features. "Willy! Pedro! Get some ropes. I want these two tied up real tight!" He chuckled gleefully. "Are we gonna have some fun with you!"

"That's what I'm afraid of," Lex said under her breath.

6

"But I told you before!" Jeff whined, his beard quivering. "I don't know where they'd take your friend!"

"You must have some idea," Blade said. They were parked next to the curb on Clayton Boulevard, the cycle's motor idling. Several children were playing 40 yards to the east. A man and a woman were leaning against a building 20 yards from the children. None of them paid any attention to Blade and the biker. Why should they? Blade reasoned. With his leather vest, he must appear to be another Leather Knight. He had forced Jeff to stick to the side streets after they'd entered St. Louis. Once a pack of seven bikers had passed, but they'd only waved and continued riding. Blade had beamed at them and returned their wave.

"There are a bunch of places they could've taken him," Jeff said. "I wouldn't know where to start."

Blade, seated behind the biker on the cycle, placed his right hand on the Leather Knight's right shoulder and squeezed.

Jeff flinched and cringed.

Blade allowed his steely fingers to relax. "I'm losing my patience," he informed Jeff. "I don't care where you start looking, but you had better start right now!"

Jeff nodded and quickly accelerated from the curb. He traveled east on Clayton Boulevard, then made a left on Hanley Road, and shortly thereafter took a right on Delmar Boulevard.

Blade saw more and more people as they drew closer to the inner city. Most of them did not wear the distinctive black leather of the Leather Knights. He was surprised to discover St. Louis inhabited by thousands of residents, and he wondered why St. Louis had been spared a direct hit during World War III. Weren't there any primary or secondary military targets in the St. Louis area at the time of the war? He couldn't remember.

They passed four Leather Knights heading in the opposite direction.

And what about the Leather Knights? Blade asked himself. How was it the people of St. Louis allowed themselves to be dominated by the Knights? Was it the protection the Knights afforded? Or simply the fact that, according to Jeff, the Leather Knights possessed almost all of the functional firearms and an armory of other weapons?

Up ahead loomed an intersection. Jefferson Avenue, said a sign.

Blade's reverie deepened. He mentally compared the Leather Knights to his Family. In the Family, men and women equally shared the responsibilities and duties of preserving the Home and rearing children. Women were even accorded Warrior status. But here in St. Louis it was different. The women evidently lorded it over the men. Why did the men permit it? By Jeff's own admission, the men were no longer numerically inferior, as they had been immediately after the "turf wars." So why didn't the men, if they resented the treatment they were receiving, rectify the situation? Was it because, after a century of female control, the men were conditioned to accept it as an indisputable fact?

Lost in thought, Blade failed to notice the three Leather Knights parked at the side of the road, in a small grassy stretch behind a ruined truck, just past the intersection with Jefferson Avenue.

But Jeff did see them. One of them glanced in his direction, and Jeff silently formed the word "Help!" with his lips.

The Knights' eyes narrowed.

Jeff repeated his action, twisting the left corner of his mouth backwards after he mouthed the word.

Where did the Leather Knights obtain their motorcycles? Blade speculated silently. How were they able to maintain the bikes? Where did they find the spare parts and the fuel? Why didn't—

There was a loud rumble from the rear.

Blade looked over his left shoulder.

Three Leather Knights were rapidly bearing down on them.

Blade shifted in his seat. Why was the trio coming so fast? Were they on urgent business of some nature? Or did they suspect he was an imposter? Blade leaned forward. "Faster," he ordered. He peered over his shoulder again, expecting his command to be obeyed. Blade knew Jeff was intimidated by him, and he confidently disregarded the possibility of the craven biker resisting. Complacency, one of the cardinal errors a Warrior could commit, inevitably precipitated adversity. And this time was no exception.

Jeff gunned the motor and the cycle streaked forward from 40 to 50 miles an hour. When he reached 50, Jeff unexpectedly rammed his left elbow around, slamming it into Blade's side. At the same instant he jerked the cycle to the left, adding the momentum of the bike to his blow.

Caught completely unaware, Blade, one hand holding the Commando and the other loosely on Jeff's shoulder, was knocked from the bike. It happened so quickly he scarcely realized what occurred; one second he was riding the motorcycle, and the next he was on the road, his body rolling end over end to the south side of the highway. His body crashed into a hard object, his right side bearing the brunt of the impact. Stunned, he shook his head to clear the cobwebs, then urged to his feet as the true magnitude of his dilemma hit home.

The three Leather Nights, guns drawn, were 30 yards off and roaring toward him.

Jeff had accelerated after dumping Blade, and was now hightailing it to the east.

Damn!

Blade realized the Commando was still in his hands. He'd instinctively clasped it to his chest as he tumbled from the cycle. Thank the Spirit his stupidity wasn't total!

The three Leather Knights began firing. Two of them had revolvers, the third a rifle.

Blade crouched and fired a burst from the Commando.

One of the Knights screamed as his chest was cut to ribbons and he was flipped from his cycle. The bike crashed to the road and slid for 20 feet, sparks flying from underneath, before it came to a rest.

The two remaining bikers veered to the other side of the road, vanishing behind an overgrown hedge.

Doubledamn!

Blade rose and turned, scanning the nearby buildings for the best cover. His left foot caught on something and he sprawled to the ground.

What the—?

It was a peculiar object, sort of a metallic reddish mushroom, with caps of some sort on both sides and a curved top. The red paint was peeled and faded. The lower end of the object was imbedded in the concrete curb. It was the thing he'd hit after falling from the bike. What in the world was it?

A shot cracked from behind the hedge and the sidewalk near Blade's eyes was chipped by a bullet, fragments spraying outwards.

Blade felt a cement chip strike his left cheek,

drawing blood and he leaped up and ran for a large tree ten feet away.

The two Leather Knights opened up at random.

Blade reached the tree and ducked from sight. What now? He was afoot, in enemy territory, and he had no idea where Rikki was being held—if Rikki was still alive—in St. Louis, an immense city impossible for one man to adequately cover.

The Leather Knights had stopped shooting.

Maybe Hickok had been right. Maybe both of them should have ventured into the city.

Far off, to the east, appeared more bikers.

Terrific!

It was probably Jeff with reinforcements. So now he had Knights behind him and Knights in front of him.

What to do?

Blade peeked around the trunk of the tree. All was quiet in the vicinity of the hedge. He darted from the tree and raced to the corner of the street. A weather-ravaged sign indicated this was the junction of Delmar and 23rd. He jogged to his right, staying on the worn sidewalk, seeking a hiding place or somewhere he could make a stand. He lost track of the distance he ran as he took one side street after another, first in one direction, then in another, hoping to lose the Leather Knights. He could hear their bikes to his rear and to his left. They were probably conducting a sweep.

Over a dozen residents saw him run by, but none of them displayed any inclination to interfere with a bronzed giant carting a machine gun.

An alley appeared on his right, its entrance filled with rusted trash cans and other debris.

Blade paused and surveyed the street he was on. He was alone. Perfect! He hurried into the alley and slid behind a pile of moldy boxes and piled garbage.

None too soon.

Two Leather Knights thundered into view, slowly

cruising the street, each biker concentrating on one side.

Blade flattened against the west wall of the alley and tensed. Would they stop and investigate the alley?

The pair of Knights, a woman and a man, a "sister" and a "stud," drew abreast of the alley.

The woman braked.

Blade could see them through a crack between the boxes.

The woman was eyeing the alley speculatively, apparently considering whether to check it out.

The man stopped and glanced at the woman. "Come on," he said. "No one would hide in that crap."

"You never know," the woman stated. She turned off her bike and dismounted.

Blade placed his finger on the Commando's trigger.

The male Knight sighed and did the same.

Blade focused on the slim opening dividing the boxes and garbage at the mouth of the alley.

The sister drew an automatic pistol in her left hand and cautiously advanced.

The stud was ten feet behind her, his revolver still in its holster on his right hip, certain they were wasting their time.

Blade made a calculated decision. If the women ruled the Leather Knights, then one of them was his best bet for supplying the information he required.

This woman was of average height, about five feet six, and in the neighborhood of 115 pounds. She wore a black vest and black shorts, revealing an ample cleavage and very shapely legs. Her hair was a dusty blonde, her facial features lean but attractive. The automatic was aimed straight ahead and her brown eyes alertly probed the alley as she neared it.

Blade held his breath and clutched the Commando.

The woman reached the mouth of the alley. She

took a tentative step forward and glanced to the east.

Blade sprang, sweeping the Commando stock around and in, catching the Leather Knight in the abdomen.

The woman doubled over as the stock plowed into her stomach. She gasped and dropped the pistol, dazed, out of breath.

The stud's face had betrayed his astonishment as the sister was struck, and now he went for his revolver, clawing at his holster, frantically attempting to draw.

Blade, thankful his opponent lacked even a third of Hickok's speed, raised the Commando and fired over the woman's back.

His hand still striving to draw his gun, the Knight was hit in the head by the burst. His eyes and nose caved inward in a spray of red and he toppled to the street.

No time to lose!

Blade clipped the woman on her jaw as she took a step backwards. She moaned and sagged to the ground, unconscious.

If only he knew how to ride a motorcycle!

Blade knelt and lifted the woman in his brawny left arm. He effortlessly draped her over his broad shoulders and wheeled, making for the gloomy interior of the alley. His nose was assailed by absolutely revolting odors, almost prompting him to gag. Avoiding soggy mounds of garbage, his boots squishing with every step, he reached a low wall at the end of the alley. The top of the wall was six feet from the ground.

The Leather Knight groaned.

Blade slung his Commando over his right shoulder, then leaped, his arms clearing the top of the wall up to his elbows. He easily pulled himself over the brick wall, with the woman over his shoulder, and dropped to the ground on the other side.

A vacant parking lot fronted the alley wall.

Blade unslung his Commando and began walking across the lot. Tumble-down buildings bordered the parking lot on three sides, possibly former apartment dwellings now in a state of terminal decay. The north side of the lot was adjacent to a street.

Would the Leather Knights be hunting for him in this area? Or had they already done so and departed?

Blade glanced in both directions when he reached the street. Good! No one was in sight. On the other side of the street rose a three-story brick building, obviously uninhabited to judge by the number of broken windows and its grubby appearance. He jogged across the street and up a flight of cement steps to the landing. The door was slightly ajar, and he eased it open with his right foot. The hinges creaked as the door swayed outward. He crept inside, keeping his back to the wall, listening for sounds.

All was quiet.

Blade resisted an urge to sneeze. There was a lot of dust in the air and a musty scent about the place. He was in a wide hallway leading into the dim recesses of the building. A flight of stairs to the right led to the floors above.

The woman was moaning.

Blade opted for the stairs. He took three at a stride as he climbed to the third floor. This floor received considerable light through its missing or cracked windows, illuminating the rooms with a diluted, dusty haze. He entered a room providing a vista of the street below and deposited his prisoner on the floor, near the one window, propping her against the wall to the left of the sill. He took a step back and aimed the Commando at her head.

She woke up.

Blade had to admire her reaction. There wasn't a hint of fear in her brown eyes, just a trace of surprise and unconcealed defiance.

"Who the hell are you?" the blonde demanded angrily.

Blade grinned and wagged the barrel of the Commando. "I'll ask the questions, if you don't mind," he said.

The blonde shrugged. "Suit yourself, slime! You've got the upper hand, for now anyway."

"How are you feeling?" Blade asked.

She gingerly rubbed her sore chin. "I'll live, no thanks to you."

"What's your name?"

"Mel," she answered, examining him from head to toe.

"Mel? That's a strange name for a woman," Blade said.

"It's short for Melissa," Mel revealed.

"I'll get right to the point, Mel," Blade said. "I'm looking for a friend of mine, a short man dressed in black with what you might describe as Oriental features. Have you seen him?"

Mel's face tightened. "No," she responded defensively.

Blade moved the Commando closer to her facee. "You're lying. I don't have time to play games with you. Either you cooperate, or I'll take this gun and smash your teeth in."

Mel studied him a moment. "I believe you would at that," she said. "And I sure don't want to call your bluff. My teeth are important to me." She smirked and moved her mouth back and forth. "I'm lucky I have any left after that sock you gave me."

"So where is the man in black?" Blade pressed her. "Have you seen him?"

"Yep. Just a short while ago. Terza hung him and Lex out for Slither, but they escaped." Mel laughed at the memory. "No one's ever got away from Slither before! Terza was ready to shit bricks!"

"You say they escaped?" Blade inquired hopefully.

"Yes and no," Mel said.

"How do you mean?"

"They got away from Slither, but then they were caught again nearby," Mel elaborated.

"Where are they now?"

"Terza is holding them at the library. I don't know why. She probably has something special in store for your friend. Maybe she'll feed him to Grotto," Mel disclosed.

"What is this Grotto I keep hearing about?" Blade inquired.

Mel seemed to shiver. "Grotto is one of the things—you know, like Slither—those mutant things we've got all over the place."

Blade pondered for a minute. "How far are we from the library?"

"Not far," Mel said.

"How long would it take us to get there?" Blade asked.

"Not long."

"Be specific," Blade instructed her. "Fifteen minutes? A half an hour? What?"

Mel appeared to be confused. "What's a minute?" she questioned him.

Blade chuckled. He kept forgetting! People living outside the Home or the Civilized Zone existed, for the most part, in profound ignorance. Public education was a thing of the past. Few books survived because most had been destroyed in the century since World War III, many used as kindling for fires during the frigid winters. Here and there, isolated pockets of humanity retained minimal knowledge of the cultural and scientific achievements extant at the outbreak of the war. "A minute is a measure of time," Blade told her. "Don't any of the Leather Knights own a watch?"

Mel shook her head. "Nope. Should we?"

"No," Blade stated. "I guess not. It's hard to imagine a watch lasting a hundred years." A puzzling thought occurred to him. If most of the Leather Knights were as ignorant as Melissa, then how were they able to maintain their motorcycles? "About your bikes," he said.

"What about them?"

"Where do you obtain them?" Blade queried. "Where do you get them from?"

"We get them from our head when we take the oath," Mel answered.

"Your leader gives them to you when you take your oath of admittance?"

"That's what I said," Mel declared.

"But where does your leader get them from? Do you have your own mechanics?" Blade asked.

Mel nodded. "A lot of the Knights can fix their own bikes."

"Where do they learn to do it? Where do they get the parts?" Blade inquired.

"As far as fixing the bikes goes," Mel said, "we sort of pick it up from each other. The parts we get from the Technics."

"The Technics?"

"Yeah. They live up north, in a city called . . ." She paused, trying to recall the name she wanted.

"Is it a big city?" Blade goaded her. "A small city? What?"

"I've never been there," Melissa said. "But I heard it's real big. I remember something about wind . . ."

"The Windy City? Chicago?" Blade ventured.

"That's it! Chicago," Mel confirmed.

"Who are these Technics?"

"I don't know much about them," Mel said. "Except that they control a lot of turf north of us and they're very powerful."

"Why do they supply you with parts for your cycles?" Blade asked.

"Because of the pact."

"What pact?"

"There's a pact between us Knights and the Technics. They've agreed to help us out with our bikes, and we help them by controlling this territory and making sure the Reds don't get past us."

"I had a run-in with the Reds," Blade disclosed. "Who are they?"

"The Reds? They're the Commies," Mel said matter-of-factly.

"Communists? These Reds are Communists? Are they Russians?" Blade inquired in an excited tone.

"I don't know nothing about no Russians," Mel responded. "I only know we've been calling them Reds or Commies since I was a little girl. They're our enemies. They spy on us a lot with those copters of theirs, and we take potshots at them whenever we get the chance. Mostly they stay on their side of the river and we stay on ours."

"So the Communists control the land east of the Mississippi?" Blade probed.

"They control a lot of it, I hear," Mel affirmed. "The Technics control some too. And there are other groups." Her voice lowered. "The Dragons are the ones you want to avoid. I've been told stories about them you wouldn't believe!" She trembled.

"Where are these Dragons located?"

"Way to the east of here," Mel replied. " But south of the Reds."

Blade contemplated her revelations. He'd never heard of the Dragons or the Technics before. But the Communists were another matter. The Family's leaders had often wondered what happened to the Russians after the war. Why hadn't the U.S.S.R. taken over the U.S.? After the devastating nuclear exchange, not to mention all of the chemical and conventional weapons employed during the war, the remnants of the U.S. Government had evacuated the populace and reorganized their forces in the Midwest and Rocky Mountain region, locating the new capital at Denver, Colorado. They had braced for a Russian invasion, an eventuality which had never transpired. Except for vague rumors, the Russians had never materialized. The U.S. Government had devolved into a dictatorship known as the Civilized Zone, and only recently had the people of the Civilized Zone reclaimed their heritage and asserted their independence. During the intervening century, as the years rolled on and the Russians never attacked, the people in the Civilized Zone had forgotten about their former adversaries. But if, as Melissa asserted, the Russians did control a section of the U.S., then the Civilized Zone and all of the other members of the Freedom Federation must be warned! The Family, the Cavalry in the Dakota territory, the Flathead Indians in Montana and the Moles in their subterranean city in northern Minnesota must all be alerted to the Soviet presence.

Melissa was waiting for Blade to speak.

"Has anyone ever gone into Red territory?" Blade asked.

"Years ago some tried," Mel answered.

"What did they discover?"

"Nothing. They never came back," she said.

Blade stared out the window, noting the light was fading. "I want you to take me to the library where my friend is being held."

Mel started to rise.

"Not now!" Blade said. "After it's dark we'll leave."

She resettled herself on the floor. "Fine by me. But you'd be doing yourself a favor if you took off. There's no way you're going to save him."

"I've got to try."

"Any last words you want me to say when we plant you?"

7

So what the blazes was he supposed to do? Count the stars?

Still smarting at being left behind to babysit the SEAL, Hickok was seated on the highway, his back resting against the undercarriage of the transport, a canteen on the ground near his left knee. His rifle, a Navy Arms Henry Carbine in 44-40 caliber, was propped against the vehicle to his right.

Talk about boring!

The night sky was rich with stars, a fantastic display of the mightiness of creation, splendid galaxies traversing their ordained course much like the prescribed circuits of electrons on the subatomic level of reality. Hickok experienced a rare sense of awe as he admired the spectacular heavens. He recollected his schooling days at the Home, the survivalist compound in northwestern Minnesota constructed by Kurt Carpenter immediately prior to World War III. Carpenter's close-knit descendants— the Family, as they called themselves—were dedicated to insuring every child in the Home received a quality education. With the Family Elders as Teachers, the school developed self-reliant personalities with noble, moral character. Many times, Hickok remembered, he'd been told there was a grand design to the scheme of things. The Elders wisely taught there was a distinct purpose to every element of creation. Now, as he gazed at the sea of stars and was impressed by the immensity of the cosmos, Hickok began to wonder what his purpose was in life. How did he fit into the scheme of things? The only special talent he possessed was in handling firearms, especially handguns. The others might label him as too cocky, but he positively believed that nobody, but *nobody*, could match him with a revolver. His expertise was inherent, a totally unconscious aptitude on his part. The Family Elders taught thankfulness for the gifts bestowed by the Maker. Was it possible, he asked himself, his gift was his ambidextrous ability with revolvers? Was it conceivable the Maker had placed him on this planet to be exactly what he was: one of the Family's preeminent Warriors, devoted to safeguarding the Home and protecting his loved ones?

Was it likely?

Hickok shook his head, clearing his mind, bemused by his train of thought. He'd never really considered the issue much before, and now was hardly the time to start. The only reason he gave it any attention at all was because of the sermon given by the Family's spiritual sage, Joshua, shortly before his departure to St. Louis. Why was it, Hickok wondered, folks like Josh always had to analyze everything to death? Why couldn't they just accept things for what they were and leave it go at that?

The gunman chuckled. It was way over his head, that was for sure! Oh, he could recollect a few details from his Family science courses about the formation of galaxies and the formation of matter and stuff like that, but what good did it do him? All he ever wanted out of life was a cool breeze, his Colts in his hands, and his wife and son by his side.

What else mattered?

Hickok relaxed, listening to the sound of the insects and nocturnal critters emanating from the forest on both sides of the highway. There were crickets by the thousands, tree frogs, an occasional owl, and others. Once, far off in the dark depths of the woods, arose the challenging roar of some large carnivore.

Maybe this waiting wasn't so bad after all.

At least he'd catch up on his shut-eye.

The forest suddenly became quiet, absolutely silent, not a creature so much as fluttering its wings.

Hickok was instantly alert. He grabbed the Henry and rose, staring into the gloomy vegetation on his side of the highway.

The silence could only mean one thing.

Something was prowling through the woods, something deadly, something the other animals were deathly afraid of.

But what? A cougar? Was this neck of the woods part of their range? How about a bear? Or worse? One of the ravenous, mutated horrors proliferating since the Big Blast? Or the deadliest killer of all?

Man.

Hickok crouched and moved to the edge of the road, his head cocked to one side.

An unnerving hush enveloped the forest.

Was something stalking him?

The gunman flattened, knowing the lower he was, the less of an outline he presented, the less of a target he was. At night, the surest way to detect someone or something in your vicinity was to drop to the ground and scan the near horizon for the fluid movement of a figure silhouetted by the backdrop of the sky.

Nothing.

Which meant whatever was out there was lurking in the trees.

So!

Sneaky bunch of varmints!

Hickok crawled toward the treeline, his knees and elbows propelling him forward. He reached the base of a mighty oak and stood, flattening against the tree.

So far, so good!

The next move was up to whatever was out there.

A branch snapped off to his left.

Something crackled to the right.

There was definitely more than one of them!

Hickok could feel the rough bark of the tree through his buckskin shirt. A stub or a broken section of a branch was gouging his lower back.

Another twig crunched to the left.

No doubt about it! They were making too much noise to be critters. No self-respecting animal would be so klutzy sneaking up on a meal.

Had to be humans.

Or something similar.

A black form detached itself from the wall of vegetation not ten feet to Hickok's left.

A second later, a second shape did likewise on the gunman's right.

Upright.

Bipeds, as Plato would say.

Men. Or women.

Lugging lengthy sticks in their hands. Sticks . . . or guns.

Time for a surprise party!

Hickok raised the Henry and aimed at the figure to his left. The 44.40 boomed, and the shadow disappeared. He spun, sighting on the middle of the form to his right and pulling the trigger. The Henry's stock slammed into his shoulder, and the silhouette screamed as it was brutally flung backward to the turf.

Two down!

Hickok dodged behind the sheltering oak, and not a moment too soon.

A machine gun opened up from the other side of the highway, its heavy slugs biting into the tree in the exact spot the gunman had vacated.

Someone out there was a darn good shot!

Hickok darted into the brush, avoiding trees and

tangled bushes, treading carefully to avoid tripping on a rock or limb on the ground, heading deeper into the forest. The SEAL was locked up tight as the proverbial drum, and there was no way these dudes would be able to bust inside. So his best bet was to lead them on a merry chase, a chase away from the transport. Considering he was obviously outnumbered, it was the sensible thing to do. The murky forest would reduce their mobility and limit their effectiveness.

Someone was crashing through the undergrowth to his right.

Hickok fell to his knees, peering through the vegetation.

A bulky form was foolishly plowing through a thicket eight yards away.

What a cowchip!

Hickok aimed at the advancing figure and fired, the 44-40 thundering in his ears.

Cowchip screeched and dropped, uttering an awful gurgling sound as he thrashed on the ground.

Hickok kept going.

From the rear, from the direction of the SEAL, a man began barking orders.

Hickok stopped, perplexed. What language was the rascal using? It sure wasn't English. Or Spanish. It was like no language he'd ever heard before.

The underbrush was alive with the passage of black figures seeking the Warrior.

So much for catching up on his shut-eye!

Hickok reached a rocky knoll and quickly climbed to the top. A ring of small boulders furnished excellent concealment and an ideal spot to defend himself.

Let them come!

They did. Four, five, six forms slowly moving toward the knoll.

How the blazes did they know where he was?

The figures stopped and abruptly vanished.
Hickok realized they had gone to ground or were hiding behind trees or other cover.
More orders were shouted in the strange tongue.
There was a rustling and a series of metallic clicks from the woods below the knoll.
Now what?
A shadow appeared for an instant from behind the trees, and there was a loud whooshing sound.
Hickok sighted the Henry, but the form receded behind the tree before he could fire.
There was a muffled thump followed by a strange hissing noise as something struck the top of the knoll five feet below the rim.
What the blazes was going on?
Wispy smoke tendrils began filling the night air, spiraling upward, assuming the proportions of a hovering gray cloud.
More distinct whooshing sounds came from the forest below the knoll, one after the other, nine in all.
More thumping noises ringed the knoll.
The mysterious gray cloud grew bigger and bigger, completely enshrouding the knoll.
Confounded by the odd sounds and wary of the clouds, Hickok eased over the boulders and crawled toward the woods. The gray cloud descended to ground level. Caught by the smoky substance, the gunman almost gagged as he breathed in his first mouthful. An intense burning sensation erupted in his throat and chest and his eyes started watering. He coughed and held his breath, rolling down the knoll, trying to get well out of the cloud before he would need to take another breath.
Was it a poison gas of some kind?
Hickok resisted an impulse to gag, his lungs heaving. He rolled into a boulder and was jarred by the impact. Unable to control himself, he accidentally inhaled.

It was as if he had swallowed a handful of red hot coals.

Hickok doubled over as his body was rocked with painful spasms, his breathing impaired, his breaths coming in great, ragged gasps. The burning sensation in his chest increased, becoming acute, nearly unbearable.

Poison gas! It had to be!

The Warrior staggered to his feet and stumbled toward the trees. Fortunately, the lower he went the thinner the cloud became, until he reached the bottom of the knoll and clear, fresh air.

Hickok inhaled the cool, crisp air, endeavoring to pump the poison from his system.

Black figures were advancing toward him from the woods.

The lousy varmints! They couldn't take him fair and square! They had to resort to their poison gas! They may have succeeded in killing him, but they had horse patties for brains if they expected him to lie down and die without so much as a whimper of protest! By the Spirit! He'd show them what it meant to tangle with a Warrior! Despite the reluctance of his limbs to comply with his mental commands, he managed to raise the Henry.

Someone was yelling in the unfamiliar language.

Hickok squeezed the trigger, his effort rewarded by the collapse of one of the approaching forms.

That'd show the curs!

His eyes moist from his copious tears, his arms feeling leaden and burdened by the heavy Henry, Hickok opted for a change in tactics.

If it was his time to buy the farm, he might as well go in style!

Hickok dropped the Henry and drew his Pythons, his arms sluggish, his draw a mere fraction of its normal speed. His feet shuffled forward, directly at his foes.

There were more of them than he'd imagined. Ten or more, closing in from all sides.

Why weren't they shooting?

Hickok swiveled the Colts, going dead center on one of the figures. The Pythongs cracked and bucked in his unsteady hands.

Another opponent bit the dust.

Why weren't they returning his fire?

Hickok turned, wobbly, and fired his right Python.

Yet another form screamed and fell.

What was going on? Why didn't they fight back?

Hickok's ears detected a slight rustling behind him, and he tried to swing around to confront the source.

He never made it.

The gunman felt a hard object slam into his head, and he was knocked forward onto his hands and knees. He wheezed as he struggled to stand, but before he could rise someone leaped onto his back and strong hands gripped his blonde locks and yanked.

Hickok grunted as his head was snapped backwards.

What were they trying to do? Break his neck?

Something soft and reeking of an obnoxious odor was pressed over the gunman's nostrils and mouth.

What the—!

Hickok knew they were expecting him to try and stand, to toss the attacker from his back. Instead, he did the opposite, allowing his body to pitch forward, hoping the unexpected motion would dislodge or disorient the person on his back.

He was right.

The man on the gunman's back lost his hold and toppled to the left.

Hickok rolled to the right, extending his Colts.

There was more shouting in the weird lingo.

A bulky form reared above the Warrior.

Hickok let the vermin have it. Both Pythons from

point-blank range.

The blurry figure was hurtled backward by the impact.

Hickok rose to his knees, relieved because his vision was beginning to return.

They converged on the gunman in a rushing mass, piling on him from everywhere. Powerful hands grabbed his arms and legs. Someone had him by the hair again.

Hickok was knocked onto his back. A knee rammed into his stomach. Fingers were tugging on the Colts, striving to strip them from his hands. The obnoxious odor penetrated his nostrils as the soft material was again pressed over his mouth and nose.

What were they doing?

Hickok thrashed and heaved for all he was worth, knowing he was dead if he didn't break free.

There were simply too many of them.

The gunman's last thoughts were of his wife and son.

8

"On your feet. It's time to leave."

"You'll never make it."

"You let me worry about that," Blade said. He gazed out the window at the night sky. Darkness had enveloped the city long ago. Lacking public utilities, St. Louis was plunged into an inky abyss. The towering skyscrapers seemed like brooding monoliths. Streets and alleys resembled lighter ribbons in a tapestry of black fabric. All outside activity ceased as residents took to their dwellings, families to their homes and singles, for the most part, to their apartments. After he had questioned Mel, Blade had learned more concerning the Leather Knights and their domination of St. Louis. Because structurally sound houses were at a premium, the Knights had ruled only families could reside in individual homes. The single men and women tended to live in clusters, in apartment buildings relatively unscathed by the ravages of time and the elements.

Blade glanced down at the woman. "Take me directly to the library where they are holding my friend. One false move and I'll slit your throat."

"You sure have a way with the ladies," Melissa quipped.

Blade stepped away from the window and motioned with the Commando. "Let's go."

Melissa slowly stood, her legs cramped from her prolonged sitting.

"Do the Knights patrol the streets at night?" Blade asked.

"Yeah," Mel replied. "But the patrols are few and far between."

"I would think you'd want to insure the Reds don't sneak into the city after dark," Blade said. "You must have a lot of patrols."

Mel snickered. "After dark? Are you nuts? The . . . things . . . come out after dark. The Reds aren't any more likely than we are to run around at night. It's bad enough having to look out for the mutants in the daytime. At night it's worse because you can't see them coming."

"Haven't you cleared them out of the city?" Blade inquired.

"We've tried," Mel answered. "But it's not that easy. The giant rats are impossible to control. There are too many of them. Some of the things, like Slither and Grotto, are too big to handle. And although we can keep many of the monsters out during the day, some of them sneak back into the city at night looking for food. Most people stay inside at night with their doors locked. And one of the first rules you learn as a child is this: never go outside at night alone." She paused. "No, you don't have to worry about running into anybody this late at night."

"Good. Then we should reach the library without any problem," Blade said.

"Yeah," Mel cracked. "Unless we run into one of the . . . things."

"I'll protect you," Blade assured her.

"I hope so," Melissa stated. "Being eaten alive by one of those ugly suckers isn't high on my list of things to do."

Blade nodded toward the doorway. "Walk slowly. And remember what I told you. Don't try anything funny."

Mel moved to the doorway, stopped, peered into

the hallway, then walked from the room.

Blade stayed glued to her heels.

They descended the stairs to the ground floor and reached the front door.

Melissa hesitated, her right hand on the doorknob.

"Let's go," Blade goaded her.

Mel took a deep breath, squared her shoulders, and opened the door.

The night air was cool and crisp.

Blade followed the Leather Knight as she hurried down the cement steps to the street and took a left. She kept to the middle of the streets as she proceeded into the murky bowels of St. Louis, constantly scanning the surrounding buildings for any hint of movement or the slightest sound. He lost track of the route they took. The few remaining street signs were vague markers impossible to read in the eerie gloom. Ominous rustling noises and scratching sounds emanated from gutted structures and darker alleys.

Melissa drew up short as a loud hissing issued from the mouth of a gaping alley.

Blade prodded her with the Commando barrel. "Keep going."

"I don't like this," Melissa muttered nervously. "I don't like this one bit!"

Blade nudged her again. "I'm right behind you."

Mel glanced over her left shoulder. "I hope Terza feeds you to Grotto!" she snapped. She resumed their journey.

Blade stared into the impenetrable alley as he passed, but he couldn't see a thing.

The sooner they reached the library, the better!

Mel increased her pace, evidently equally anxious to reach their destination.

Headlights appeared at the far end of the street they were on.

Blade gripped Melissa's right shoulder and shoved her toward the left sidewalk. "Take cover!" he ordered.

Melissa blinked.

Blade pushed her, causing her to stumble and almost fall. "Take cover!" he repeated, his tone a threatening growl.

Melissa crossed to the sidewalk and crouched in a dim doorway.

Blade joined her, flattening his powerful frame against the right jamb. "Don't make a sound!" he warned her.

Blade ran his finger along the Commando trigger.

It was a Leather Knight patrol, five riders moving at a leisurely pace, packed close together, every one of them armed to the teeth.

Blade watched Melissa, wondering if she would betray him.

The patrol passed without incident.

Blade waited until the five bikers were out of sight to the west. "Thanks for not giving me away," he said.

Melissa rose. "Don't thank me," she said angrily. "I just didn't want to get caught in a crossfire."

Blade stepped into the street. "Okay. Lead out."

Mel frowned and took to the street again.

Blade's mind drifted. Even after he freed Rikki, he was still facing a major problem—namely, how to raise the SEAL to an upright position. If the transport weren't flat on its side, he might be able to use leverage by inserting a huge board or limb between the SEAL and the ground. But as it was, leverage was impractical. Then how could they manage it? Without the vehicle, none of the Warriors would be able to return to the Home. The distance was too great and the dangers insurmountable.

There must be a way!

Melissa led the Warrior ever inward, block after circuitous block. The gigantic skyscrapers blotted out the stars overhead. Instead of being freshly invigorating, the night air became dank and foul. The residents of St. Louis were not meticulous about their personal or civic hygiene; piles of rotting garbage and rodent-infested trash filled most of the alleys.

Just when Blade began to doubt the Leather Knight was really leading him to the library, she stopped and coughed.

"There it is," Mel said, pointing across the street.

Blade could distinguish a huge building about 20 yards off, utterly devoid of life and light. "There aren't any guards," he whispered suspiciously.

"Why should there be?" Mel countered. "Who'd want to break into the library? There's nothing there but a few moldy books."

"But what about keeping your prisoners from breaking out?" Blade asked.

Melissa laughed. "No way."

"You're that confident?"

"No one busts out,' Mel assured him.

"You don't know Rikki-Tikki-Tavi," Blade said.

Melissa took a step away. "Well, you won't be needing me any longer."

Blade covered her with the Commando. "Yes, I will."

"But I brought you here like you wanted," she protested.

"Now you'll take me to where they're holding my friend," Blade told her.

"And what if I don't?" Mel challenged him. "What are you gonna do. Shoot me? The noise will attract the others."

Blade patted his left Bowie. "I could always use this," he said. "Or this," he added, touching Rikki's katana.

Melissa got the message. She turned and headed for the library, moving cautiously, manifestly nervous.

Blade sensed something was wrong. She had been antsy on the way here, true, but not like this. She was acting . . . different. Had she lied? Were there guards posted outside the library? Was she attempting to lead him into an ambush? Was it likely to—

A machine gun opened up from the direction of the library.

"No!" Melissa screamed, throwing her arms up. "It's me! Mel! Don't shoot!"

Her cry came too late.

The street around them was struck by a zigzag pattern of slugs.

Blade heard Mel grunt as she was hit. She doubled over and fell forward, and in that instant he spotted the flash of the gunner hiding at the top of the library steps.

So! She had tried to trap him!

Blade was caught in the open. If he endeavored to reach cover, the guard would have ample opportunity to fill him with lead. In the microsecond it took him to perceive the threat and evaluate his position, Blade decided on the timeworn couse of action proven in innumerable conflicts: the best defense is invariably a good offense. He charged the library, weaving back and forth, firing from the hip, going for the gunflash on the library steps.

A bullet nicked his left thigh.

Blade executed a diving leap for the tarmac, scraping his elbows and the katana's scabbard as he rolled to the left and came up on his knees, the Commando pointed at the library stairs. He fired a burst in a sweeping arc.

Someone shrieked, and a moment later a woman toppled from the deeper shadows at the top of the steps and tumbled to the sidewalk.

Damn!

They'd probably aroused every Leather Knight in St. Louis!

Blade rose and ran to the prone form on the sidewalk. The woman had been shot in the chest and was oozing blood from a cavity where her right breast had once been. He turned and raced up the stairs to the glass doors.

Please let them be open!

He gripped one of the handles and yanked, and was rewarded by the door flinging outward.

The interior of the library was, if anything, even darker than the outside.

Where the hell would Rikki be?

Blade ran down a wide corridor, his footsteps creating a hollow echo as he pounded from door to door, his boots smacking on the tiles, searching for his fellow Warrior. Four doors opened into stark offices. The fifth revealed a massive chamber filled with bookshelves. Most of the shelves were empty.

Where could he be? Had Melissa lied about Rikki being here? He didn't have much time! The other Knights were certain to investigate the gunfire and discover Melissa and the dead guard.

Where?

Blade reached a stairwell and, on a hunch, darted into it and began descending to the lower levels of the library. If the Leather Knights had converted a portion of the library into a dungeon or jail, logic dictated the holding cells might be located in the basement.

If the library even had a basement!

Blade reached a landing and paused, listening.

The night was deathly quiet.

Strange.

They should have found the bodies by now. Why wasn't there an uproar, or at least the sounds of pursuit?

Very strange.

Blade opened the landing door and found himself in a dingy hallway. It branched to the left and the right.

Terrific!

Which branch should he take?

Blade opted for the right branch and jogged along the hallway until he reached a closed door. He grabbed the doorknob, tensed, and pushed the door open.

Another damn office!

Annoyed, Blade continued his hunt. He ran another 15 yards and spied a door to his left. The doors, constructed of wood and painted or stained a pale yellow, stood out against the gloomy hallway walls.

Here goes nothing!

Blade shoved the door open.

Bingo!

This room gave every indication of being a recent fabrication. The walls were made from brick, and the floor was barren dirt. A musty scent permeated the chamber. The room was circular, perhaps 30 feet in diameter. And secured to the far wall across from the doorway, their arms locked in chains, were a man and a woman.

Rikki and another.

Blade easily recognized his small companion, despite the lack of light.

"Rikki!" Blade called. "Are you all right?"

There was a muffled noise from the other side of the chamber.

Blade took a step forward. He could see Rikki and the woman thrashing, striving to slip free from their chains, and he could hear the chains clanking against the brick wall. There was black patches over Rikki's and the woman's mouths.

They were gagged!

"Hang on!" Blade yelled. "I'll have you out of there in no time."

The huge Warrior started toward the hapless pair. He reached the center of the room.

Rikki-Tikki-Tavi was surging against his chains like a madman.

"Calm down!" Blade said. "I'm almost there! I'll get you out."

"No, you won't," said a harsh feminine voice from above.

Even as Blade glanced upward, something heavy fell onto his broad shoulders and covered his arms and torso, pinning his arms to his sides, rendering the Commando useless.

Light flooded the chamber.

A net! He was snared in a net!

Blade caught a glimpse of a balcony encircling the room, a balcony swarming with Leather Knights. He strained his arms, attempting to loosen the net, to bring the Commando into play.

His effort was wasted.

Leather Knights, men and women, poured into the chamber through three recessed doorways. They rushed to the middle of the chamber and tackled the Warrior, tightening the net until movement was impossible.

Blade, mentally berating his stupidity, wound up flat on his back staring through the strands of the nylon net at a dozen hostile faces. Now he knew what Rikki had been trying to do: warn him about the trap.

The Leather Knights parted and a brunette bearing a scar under her right eye appeared, standing over the Warrior's head. She was grinning in triumph. "Ain't you the big one?" she asked playfully.

Blade refused to respond.

"The name is Terza," she said. "And you must be the friend of Lex's hunk! Am I right?"

Lex's hunk?

Terza chuckled. "The strong, silent type, huh? Fine. There's no need to talk right now. You'll do enough talking later. I can promise you that!" She paused, then kicked the net with her right foot. "Not bad, eh? Jeff told us all about you. We knew you were coming in to save your buddy. Did you think we'd let you walk right in here and take him?"

Blade didn't answer. He was feeling monumentally dumb.

"If so," Terza continued, "you ain't as bright as you look." She laughed. "Why don't you get a good night's sleep, and we'll get down to cases in the morning." She glanced at a man with a blue Mohawk. "Cardew, why don't you tuck him in?"

"My pleasure" Cardew replied.

Blade saw the biker named Cardew walk beyond his line of vision. What was the Knight planning to do?

"Nighty-night!" Cardew said, from just beyond Blade's head.

What the—

Something crashed into Blade's face, something hard, smashing his right cheek and jarring his jaw.

Blade heaved, his arms bulging, vainly attempting to remove the net.

"One more time," Cardew stated.

The bastard must be using a club! Blade tried to roll to the left, away from Cardew's blow.

They mustn't knock him out! If they succeeded, they'd disarm him! He'd be at their mercy! They'd be . . .

9

He thought he was going to puke!

The gunman felt as if he were bobbing on the surface of a lake. Nausea engulfed him. His stomach was contracting, threatening to expel the venison jerky he'd consumed earlier.

Where the blazes was he?

What was that weird noise?

His eyelids fluttered open, and he glimpsed men in uniform seated on both sides of him. Brown uniforms with red stars on the collars. Who were they? He couldn't seem to focus, to concentrate. Why? He closed his eyes and drifted into dreamland.

10

Dear Spirit! How he hurt!

Blade's senses responded sluggishly as he struggled to regain consciousness. He vividly recalled being clobbered by the Leather Knight called Cardew, and as his eyes opened and a wave of agony washed over his head he inadvertently flinched, expecting to be struck again.

But Cardew was gone. And so were the others. The circular chamber was empty except for the nylon net in the middle of the dirt floor.

"Welcome back to the land of the living," said someone to his left.

Blade slowly turned, discovering his arms in chains.

Rikki-Tikki-Tavi was shackled to the brick wall not four feet away. He had succeeded in slipping the gag from his mouth. Beyond him hung a redheaded woman with her gag still in place.

Was she the woman named Lex?

Rikki scanned the balcony to insure it was unoccupied. "Is Hickok with you?" he asked in a low voice.

Blade shook his head and immediately regretted the movement. The right side of his face was lanced by an acute pain. "I came alone," he mumbled through swollen lips.

"I noticed you found my katana," Rikki stated.

Blade looked down. The Leather Knights had stripped all of his weapons: the Bowies, the

Commando, the katana, everything.

"They took them last night," Rikki revealed, accurately deducing Blade's train of thought, "after Cardew knocked you out. I saw them carry my sword away." He paused, his jaw muscles taut. "I intend to retrieve it."

Blade tried to speak, but his throbbing mouth balked at the effort. What had that bastard Cardew done to him? He licked his puffy lips and mustered his resolve. "Do you . . ." He said haltingly, "have . . . any idea what they plan to do with us?"

Rikki nodded. "Their leader, Terza, wants to know who we are and where we come from. She wants to question us."

"She'll be wasting her breath," Blade muttered.

Rikki glanced at the closed doors. "Why did you come in alone?" he inquired. "Why didn't you use the SEAL?"

"It's out of commission," Blade said.

"What?" Rikki asked in surprise. "How?"

"A Red copter," Blade explained.

"Can the SEAL be salvaged?" Rikki queried.

"I think so," Blade said. "It's lying on its side, but otherwise seems to be in working order. I left Hickok behind to watch over it."

"At least *he's* out of danger," Rikki commented.

"Now all we have to do is get our butts out of here," Blade remarked.

Rikki rattled the chains secured to his wrists. "Easier said than done."

One of the recessed doors abruptly opened, and in walked Terza, Cardew, and six other Knights, four of them women. All of them bore handguns.

"Morning, Turkey!" Terza greeted Blade, her attitude cheerful, her bearing haughty.

Blade glared at his captors.

Terza walked up to the strapping Warrior and grinned. "My! My! Didn't you wake up on the wrong side of the sack!" She cackled. "Didn't you sleep well?" She reached up and slapped his right cheek.

Blade recoiled in anguish.

"What a wimp!" Cardew said disdainfully.

Blade lunged at the biker with the blue Mohawk, but his chains prevented him from moving more than a few inches.

Cardew retreated a step and reached for his Browning.

"Cardew!" Terza barked. "I want him alive."

Cardew's mouth curled back from his teeth. "Okay," he hissed. "But I want the honor of wasting this creep when the time comes."

"You'll have it," Terza assured him.

Cardew snickered maliciously.

Terza moved over to Rikki. "So? Are you ready to spill the beans yet?"

"What kind of beans did you have in mind?" Rikki countered. "Lima or string beans?"

"Funny boy, ain't you?" Terza said. "Okay. I tried to be nice about this. But if you won't tell me where you come from, then I'll have to persuade you to talk."

"I will not answer your questions," Rikki assured her.

"We'll see about that, lover boy." Terza turned and nodded at two of the women. They crossed to Lex, and one of them unlocked her shackles while the second kept her covered with a revolver.

Lexine rubbed her sore wrists, then removed the gag from her mouth. "You bitch!" she snapped at Terza.

Terza motioned toward the center of the chamber. "Set her up."

The two women grabbed Lex by the arms and hauled her from the room.

"What are you going to do to her?" Rikki asked.

"You'll see," Terza replied.

Blade surveyed the chamber, lit by a dozen lanterns positioned at regular intervals along the balcony, affixed to metal brackets. Where did the Knights obtain the fuel for the lanterns? From the Technics? The ceiling was vaulted, constructed of polished wood. Evidently this chamber had been under construction at the outset of World War III and never finished.

Lex and the pair of Knights appeared on the balcony on the far side of the room. One of the women was carrying a coiled rope.

"You sure you don't wanna tell me everything I want to know?" Terza asked Rikki.

Rikki remained silent.

Terza shrugged. "Suit yourself. But I think you're about to change your mind."

One of the Knights on the balcony tied the rope to the balcony railing, then turned and said something to Lexine.

Rikki saw Lex shake her head

The second Knight shoved her revolver into Lexine's stomach.

Lex walked to the edge of the balcony. She held her arms straight out.

The Knight with the rope used it to bind lex's wrists.

"Last chance," Terza said, mocking Rikki.

Rikki resembled a granite statue.

"Do it!" Terza shouted to the two women on the balcony.

The Knights seized Lex and forced her to the edge of the balcony. Lex fought them, striving to wrest her arms free, but she was unable to avert their intended design; she was rudely jerked off her feet and pushed over the balcony railing. She dropped like the proverbial rock, her descent brutally terminated when she reached the end of the rope, her feet dangling five feet above the earthen floor. She gasped in torment as her arms were wrenched upwards, her head snapping back, whiplashed, and her teeth jarring together.

"The fun's just getting started," Terza said to Rikki. "You can put a stop to it by telling me where you come from. What do you say?"

Rikki looked Terza in the eyes. "If it's the last act I live to perform on this planet," he said calmly, "I am going to eliminate you."

"Tough talk!" Terza said, chuckling. She slowly drew the Llama Super Comanche V's belted around her slim waist. "You know what to do!" she yelled to the Knights on the balcony.

The pair of Knights leaned over the railing, gripped the rope, and started moving the rope in wide arcs, back and forth, causing Lex to swing like a human pendulum.

Terza aimed her left Comanche and fired.

The brick wall beyond Lex sprayed chipped mortar and brick onto the floor.

"Damn!" Terza said, laughing. "I missed." She stared at Rikki. "One more time. Where do you come from?"

Rikki frowned and lowered his gaze.

Terza pointed the Comanches in the direction of Lex. "I thought you had the hots for Lex, lover boy," she said. The Comanches boomed, the twin shots narrowly missing Lex's swaying form. "I guess I was wrong."

Rikki stared at the dirt floor, struggling to restrain his seething emotions. Maintaining his self-control was of paramount importance: self-control was the essence of a Warrior's character, and exhibiting self-control during a crisis was the critical test of anyone dedicated to the martial arts. He quivered from the intensity of his fury, but his inner discipline was superlative.

"Sooner or later," Terza said, baiting him, "one of

my shots is bound to hit her. Won't it bother you knowing you're responsible for her death?"

Rikki's fists were clenched so tightly his nails were digging into his palms.

Terza's right Comanche thundered, but again Lex was spared any injury.

"Let me try," Cardew interjected eagerly.

"What do you say, lover boy?" Terza asked Rikki. "Should I let Cardew have a go at it? He's not as good a shot as I am. He'll probably put a bullet right between her eyes."

Rikki glared at Cardew.

"Still the tough guy?" Terza said to Rikki. "Well, don't say I didn't warn you." She looked at Cardew. "Have some fun."

"Thanks!" Cardew drew his Browning.

"Enough of this!" declared a deep voice.

All eyes focused on the muscular giant.

"Did you say something?" Terza asked.

"Enough of this," Blade reiterated. "I'll answer your questions."

Terza studied him quizzically. "You will, huh?"

"I will answer whatever I can," Blade said.

"Just like that?" Terza remarked skeptically.

Blade nodded toward Lex. "Release her first."

Terza snickered. "Don't tell me that you've got the hots for Lex too? What's she got that I ain't got?"

Blade straightened. "I do not have the . . . hots . . . for her. I already have selected my mate for eternity."

"Eternity?" Terza laughed. "Who said anything about eternity? I figure you want to jump her buns for a one-nighter."

Blade's mouth curled downward disdainfully. "I also have no desire to jump her . . . buns. I have pledged loyalty to my wife, and I will not violate my vow."

"Yeah. Sure." Terza tittered. "Big words, mister. But they don't mean crap! Are you tryin' to tell me you would say no if a fox wanted some fun in the sack with you?"

Blade nodded. "The only fox I want to have fun with is my wife. We are loyal to one another because we love each other."

"Loyalty?" Terza said angrily. "Who the hell cares about loyalty?"

"Loyal couples are growing couples," Blade stated. "Without loyalty, love withers and dies."

"What the hell are you? Some kind of poet?" Terza shook her head in wonder.

"Sounds like a real wimp to me," Cardew commented.

"What's it going to be?" Blade demanded. "Will you release Lex?"

Terza holstered her Comanches. "Sure. But remember one thing. I can have her strung up again if you give me any grief."

"I have given my word," Blade reminded her.

"Your word don't mean diddly to me," Terza said. She raised her face to the two Knights on the balcony. "Cut her down! Then chain her on the wall next to lover boy!" She grinned at Blade. "Satisfied?"

"Ask your questions," Blade said.

"Not here," Terza said. She glanced at Cardew. "I want you to bring him to my room after Lex is chained. I'll be waiting." She wheeled and stalked from the chamber.

Cardew walked up to Blade and winked conspiratorially. "Ain't you the lucky one!"

"What do you mean?" Blade inquired.

"Don't play innocent with me!" Cardew nudged the Warrior in the ribs. "I think Terza wants you for herself. You should be flattered."

"Wants me?" Blade repeated, puzzled. "But I just told her I already have a mate."

"Terza could care less about your mate," Cardew disclosed. "If she decides she wants a man, she ups and takes him."

"And the man doesn't have any say in the matter?" Blade queried.

"A man can't refuse a woman," Cardew said. "That's the law."

"Not where I come from," Blade informed him.

"You ain't there now, are you?" Cardew teased the Warrior. "You're here. And what Terza says, goes. If you give her any lip, you'll never see your wife again. No man has ever refused her. Am I getting through to you yet, asshole?"

"Loud and clear," Blade responded. He watched the Knights lowering Lex to the ground. How were they going to get out of this fix? Would Terza want to be alone with him? If so, would it be to his advantage to escape while Rikki and Lex were still being held? Terza might execute them out of sheer spite. He closed his eyes and sighed. At least Hickok was free. He hoped he could rely on the gunman's customary impatience. Let's see. Hickok had agreed to stay with the SEAL for three days. But would the gunfighter wait that long? Highly unlikely. One day, definitely. Two, possibly. But never for three. Hickok would come looking for them, but not for another day and a half, minimum.

A lot could happen in a day and a half.

Blade opened his eyes and stared at Cardew's leering expression.

Yes, sir.

A whole lot.

And none of it good.

11

"Not now, honey," Hickok mumbled. "I'm plumb tuckered out." He rolled over and started to fall asleep again, but Sherry wouldn't leave him alone. She was insistently shaking his right shoulder. Funny thing about wives. Before the marriage, they were all over your body and coudn't seem to get enough. Then it was "I do," and "Whoa, there, buckaroo!" "Not tonight! I've got a headache!" Except when *they* were in the mood. Then the man had best be able to get it up, or it was cold stares and leftovers until the woman decided the man had repented enough for another go. Contrary critters, those females! Sherry was shaking harder now.

Hickok eased onto his back and opened his eyes.

Uh-oh.

It wasn't Sherry standing over him. It was three men, all wearing brown uniforms with red stars on their collars and other insignia.

Hickok suddenly remembered everything in a rush, and he automatically reached for his Colts. But his fingers closed on empty holsters.

They'd taken his Pythons!

One of the men, a burly man with sagging cheeks, a protruding chin, and bright blue eyes, held the Pythons aloft in his right hand. "Are these what you are looking for?" he asked in clipped, precise English.

Hickok started to rise, but the other two men had already drawn automatics from holsters on their right hips.

"Please," said the first man, evidently an officer, "don't do anything foolish. We have no intention of harming you."

"Then what am I doin' here?" Hickock demanded. "And where the blazes am I?" He rose on his elbows and scanned his surroundings, finding himself on a metal table in a well-lit room. Four overhead lights provided ample illumination. A row of equipment—medical equipment, if he guessed right—was lined up along one of the walls.

"We will ask the questions," said the burly officer. "What is your name?"

"Annie Oakley."

The officer's blue eyes narrowed. "That is a woman's name."

"Would you believe Calamity Jane?"

"Another woman's name," the burly officer remarked. "What kind of game are you playing?"

"Poker," Hickock said.

One of the other men began speaking to the burly officer in a foreign tongue.

Hickok listened intently, but couldn't make hide nor hair of their babble.

"Ahhh. I see," the burly officer said in English. "Lieutenant Voroshilov informs me you refer to a period in American history hundreds of years ago. Is this not true?"

Hickock glanced at Lieutenant Voroshilov, a youthful officer, in his 30s, with green eyes and crew-cut blond hair. "Don't tell me. Voroshilov is partial to readin' about the Old West!"

The burly officer shook his head. "Not exactly. But Lieutenant Voroshilov does have what you call a . . ." He paused for a moment. "Photographic memory. He read a book once about the history of cowboys and Indians, or some such silliness, and never forgot what he read."

"Photographic memory, huh?" Hickok said. "Then he should have smarts enough to know who you jokers are and where the dickens I am."

Burly Butt smiled. "Please forgive my rudeness. I should have introduced myself. I am General Malenkov."

"Malenkov. Voroshilov. With names like that, it's a cinch I ain't in the Civilized Zone," Hickok quipped, alluding to the area in the Midwest and Rocky Moutain region occupied by the remnant of the U.S. Government after World War III.

"Are you from the Civilized Zone?" General Malenkov asked.

"Didn't you ever hear about what curiosity did to the cat?" Hickok countered.

General Malenkov's facial muscles tightened. "I have tried to be polite, but you will not cooperate. If you will not supply the information I need willingly, then I will use other methods."

"Give it your best shot," Hickok taunted him.

General Malenkov smiled. "I will." He barked a series of orders at Lieutenant Voroshilov. That worthy wheeled and stalked to the row of medical equipment. The third, unnamed, soldier kept his pistol trained on the man in buckskins.

"What are you aimin' to do?" Hickok inquired nonchalantly.

"We will inject you with a substance our chemists developed for recalictrant subjects," General Malenkov answered.

"What's it do?"

"It is a truth serum," General Malenkov explained. "Once injected, you will divulge everything we want to know."

Hickok watched Voroshilov remove a hypodermic needle from a glass cabinet. He didn't like this one bit. It didn't take a genius to figure out who these bozos were. He'd attended the history classes in the

Family school, and he knew about the Russians and the part they'd played in the Big Blast. Who else could these clowns be?

Voroshilov was filling the hypodermic from a small vial.

Hickock calculated the risks. If they injected him with the truth serum, he'd probably spill the beans about the Family and the Home and the whole shebang. But if he went along with them for a spell, he might be able to withhold information crucial to the safety of the Family and essential to the Freedom Federation.

Lieutenant Voroshilov had finished filling the hypodermic needle. He turned and returned to the metal table.

"You don't need to go to all this trouble on my account," Hickok said.

"It's no trouble," General Malenkov assured him.

"I'll answer your questions," Hickok declared.

"Why have you changed your mind so quickly?" General Malenkov inquired.

"I'm fickle," Hickok responded. "Ask anybody. They'll tell you I never know if I'm comin' or goin'."

General Malenkov smiled, but the smile lacked any trace of genuine friendliness. His eyes were impassive pools of indeterminate intent. He said something in what Hickock assumed was Russian to Voroshilov. The lieutenant retraced his steps to the glass cabinet and replaced the hypodermic.

Hickok trusted the general about as far as he could toss a black bear. He instinctively sensed the general was up to something, but he didn't have the slightest idea what it might be. General Malenkov had acceded too readily to not using the truth serum. Why? What did the tricky bastard have up his sleeve?

"Tell us your name," General Malenkov demanded.

"Hickok." He abruptly realized Malenkov wasn't

holding his Colts.

Lieutenant Voroshilov interjected several sentences in Russian.

General Malenkov frowned. "Why do you persist in these games?"

"I told you the truth," Hickok said. "My name is Hickok. I know it's a name from the Old West. That's why I took it. It's the name of an old gunfighter I admire a lot."

General Malenkov reflected for a minute. "All right. I will give you the benefit of the doubt. For now. Where are you from, Hickok?"

"Montana," Hickok lied. Actually, the Family resided in northwestern Minnesota.

"You are far from home," General Malenkov observed.

"We were on our way to St. Louis when your men jumped me," Hickok detailed.

"Why St. Louis?"

Hickok hesitated. The general had to know about the Civilized Zone. How much more did the Russians know? Were they aware of the existence of the Cavalry in the Dakota Territory? What about the Flathead Indians or the Moles? "We were sent to see if it's inhabited," he said.

"Who sent you?"

"The Government of the Civilized Zone," Hickok fibbed again.

"I have heard of the Civilized Zone," General Malenkov said slowly. "What do you know about it?"

"Not a bunch," Hickok replied. "I know the Government of the United States reorganized in Denver after the war, and they evacuated thousands of folks from all across the country into the Midwest and Rocky Mountain area. Later it became known as the Civilized Zone."

"And you do not live there?"

"I told you," Hickok said, enjoying their verbal

sparring, their game of cat and mouse. "I live in Montana."

"Why would someone from Montana be on a mission for the Government of the Civilized Zone?" General Malenkov asked.

"My people have a treaty with 'em," Hickok revealed. "They sent us because we have the best vehicle."

"I was told about your vehicle," General Malenkov stated with interest. "A most unusual vehicle too, I might add. Where did you obtain it?"

"It was left for us by the man who founded our Home," Hickok replied. "He spent millions building the contraption, then had it secreted in a special vault until we decided we needed it."

"I intend to retrieve your vehicle," General Malenkov declared.

"It won't be easy," Hickok said. "Didn't your men tell you about the fight we had with your helicopter?"

"One of our helicopters," the general corrected the gunman. "Another of our helicopters transported our commando unit to the site and captured you, a larger version than the one you saw. I am having one of our bigger helicopters outfitted to bring your vehicle here."

"What are you aimin' to do?" Hickok joked. "Take it apart, fly the pieces here, then put it back together again?"

"No," General Malenkov said. "Our helicopter will use a winch and a sling and fly it here."

"Fly the SEAL?" Hickok laughed. "You're crazy! It weighs tons."

"The SEAL? Is that what you call it?" General Malenkov inquired.

Hickok wanted to sew his lips shut. Of all the green-horn mistakes! He'd gone and blurted out the name of the SEAL without realizing what in tarnation he was doing! What an idiot! "Yeah," he had to agree. "We call our buggy the SEAL."

"Interesting," General Malenkov remarked. "And I am not crazy. Our tandem helicopters can transport over fifteen tons. By tomorrow morning, my crew will be at the site. Believe me, our helicopters can easily bear the load of conveying your SEAL. You don't seem to know much about helicopters."

"I don't," Hickok admitted. "I never even saw one before the fight we had with that copter of yours."

"Odd. Don't they utilize helicopters in the Civilized Zone?" General Malenkov innocently inquired.

What was the general up to? Probing for secrets concerning the Civilized Zone's military capabilities? "I wouldn't know," Hickok answered "I haven't spent a lot of time in the Civilized Zone. But I did see a flying contraption of theirs once," he added. "Something called a jet."

General Malenkov's interest heightened. "A jet? What type of jet?"

Hickok shrugged. "Beats me. I don't know jets from turnips. It flew real fast, and it could fire machine guns and rockets." He didn't bother to mention the jet had been destroyed, downed in a battle with the SEAL.

General Malenkov and Lieutenant Voroshilov exchanged looks. The obviously considered the news of the jet important.

"Did you see other military hardware in the Civilized Zone?" General Malenkov queried.

Hickok repressed an impulse to laugh. The general was totally transparent; he was milking the gunman for critical tactical information. But why? Were the Russians planning to invade the Civilized Zone? If so, why now? Why had they waited so long after the war? "I saw a heap of trucks and jeeps and a tank," Hickok stated.

"Do you know any more?" General Malenkov goaded him. "How large a standing Army they maintain, for instance? What shape their weapons and equipment are in? Where their outposts are situated?"

"Nope," Hickok replied. "Like I told you, I haven't spent much time in the Civilized Zone."

General Malenkov studied the gunman for a moment. "You said your people live in Montana?"

"Yep," Hickok said, confirming his lie.

"Do they have a name?"

"No," Hickok fibbed again.

"What about the name of the town you live in?" General Malenkov pressed the issue.

"We don't live in a town," Hickok said, telling the truth for once. "We have our own compound and we keep pretty much to ourselves."

"Could you pinpoint its location on a map?" General Malenkov asked.

"Sure," Hickok responded.

"We will bring one here later," General Malenkov informed him.

"Do you mind if I ask a question?" Hickok politely inquired.

"What is it?" General Malenkov asked.

"Who are you guys? Where do you come from? And where am I?" Hickok swept the medical room with his right hand. "Where is this place?"

General Malenkov nodded. "Fair is fair," he said. "You have answered me, so I will answer you. Perhaps you will the better understand the nature of your dilemma, and you will realize why resistance is futile. You must continue to cooperate with us. You have no other choice."

Hickok sat up on the metal table.

"As you have undoubtedly guessed," General Malenkov declared, "we are professional soldiers in the Army of the Union of Soviet Socialist Republics."

"You're a long ways from home too," Hickok quipped.

General Malenkov paused. "True," he said sadly. "We are far from the Motherland." He sighed and stared at red drapes covering one of the walls. "As to your location," he said slowly, "a demonstration will be far more eloquent than mere words."

Lieutenant Voroshilov and the third soldier moved aside, clearing a path between the metal table and the drapes.

General Malenkov beckoned toward the drapes. "Go ahead. Take a look."

Hickok slid from the metal table. He noticed the general had placed his Colt Pythons on a wooden stand about four feet from the table.

"Open the drapes," General Malenkov directed the gunman.

Hickok walked to the right side of the drapes and found several cords descending from the traverse rods. He gripped the first cord and pulled.

Nothing happened.

Hickok tried the second of the three cords.

The drapes didn't budge.

What the heck was going on here? Some of the cabins at the Home were outfitted with drapes, and he knew how to work them. He pulled on the final cord.

With a swish, the red drapes parted, opening wide, revealing a picture window and a spectacular view.

It took a minute to register. Hickok had seen pictures of the scene in the photographic books in the Family library. But he'd never expected to actually *be* there.

It was impossible!

It just couldn't be!

But there it was!

General Malenkov noted the astonishment on the gunman's features. "Your eyes do not deceive you," he said.

"It can't be!" Hickok exclaimed. "It can't!"

"But it is," General Malenkov said, beaming. "It's the White House."

12

"What kept you?" Terza demanded.

Blade gaped at her, scarcely aware he was responding. "Cardew took a potty break," he wisecracked. "Must of read *War and Peace* while he was in the bathroom."

"I don't know nothin' about no *War and Peace*," Terza said. "But I do know Cardew can't read."

Blade scanned her room, which was located on the top floor of the library. Plush green carpet covered the floor, in excellent condition despite the passing of a century. The walls were covered with mahogany paneling. An easy chair and a couch were positioned directly in front of the Warrior. Beyond them, reached by climbing two small steps, was an elevated section incorporating a huge bed as its centerpiece. Terza, attired in a skimpy white-lace garment, reclined in the middle of the bed, her legs spread out, resting her head on her left hand.

"Do you like it?" Terza asked.

"I had no idea libraries in the old days were so extravagant," Blade commented.

Terza laughed. "Stupid. This was an office once. I had some of the men fix it up for me, scavenging from the abandoned stores. You'd be surprised what you can find."

"I guess I would," Blade admitted. He was perplexed by Terza's behavior. She was exhibiting none of the habitual hostility he'd observed earlier. In fact, she was going out of her way to be nice, to be friendly.

To be attractive.

Blade walked to the steps leading up to the bed. "We must talk," he told her.

Terza grinned, reached out her right hand, and patted the brown bedspread. "I didn't have you brought here to talk."

"We must talk," Blade stated.

Terza sat up. "What's the matter with you? Can't you see I have the hots for you? I don't get a craving for a man very often. You should be flattered."

"I don't seem to be getting through to you," Blade said. "I already have a wife."

"So?" Terza giggled and patted the bed again. "I'll never tell!"

Blade pondered his next move. He saw her eyes raking his body from head to toe. Something was inconsistent here. This wasn't the tough-as-nails woman he'd met. The way she was staring at him, with her nostrils flared and her eyes dilated . . .

Her eyes dilated?

Blade moved to the edge of the bed.

"Come on!" Terza urged him. "I ain't waitin' all day!"

Blade leaned over and peered into her pale blue eyes. Her pupils were expanded and unfocused, and her entire demeanor verged on inane giddiness. What was she on? Alcohol? He doubted it. Her breath lacked the telltale odor. What then? Drugs? He straightened, frowning. The Family deplored the use of drugs. For the Warriors, any addicting substance was strictly taboo. With their lives on the line daily, only a moronic jerk would distort the senses and inhibit the reflexes. Survival was frequently a matter of split-second decision-making and timing; no one on drugs would last more than a minute if confronted by a mutate, one of the monstrous giants, or any other deviate.

Drugs were plain stupid.

"Come on, handsome!" Terza said, eyeing him lecherously. She slid her left hand between her thighs. "I want it!"

"You want it?"

"Ohhhh! How I want it!" Terza cooed.

"Are you sure you want it?" Blade asked.

Terza sat up, smiling, weaving slightly. "I'm sure! Give it to me!"

Blade grinned. "If you insist."

"Do it, damnit!"

Blade hauled off and slugged her on the jaw.

Terza collapsed onto the bed, unconscious, her mouth slack, blood dribbling from her lower gum.

"Sorry about that," Blade remarked. "But I tried to warn you. Marriage without loyalty is nothing more than disguised prostitution, as our spiritual mentor, Joshua, would say. And I will never violate my oath to my mate." He shook his head, feeling foolish conducting a conversation with an unconscious woman.

Time to get the hell out of here!

Blade crossed to the door and paused. There should be a pair of guards outside the door to Terza's room. They had escorted him to the room from the basement cell. He would need to catch them by surprise. Putting a broad smirk on his face, he slowly opened the door.

There they were. Cardew and one other.

Blade glanced over his right shoulder and laughed. "Okay," he said to Terza's unresponsive form. "I'll tell them." He smiled at Cardew and the other man. "Terza wants to see you."

Cardew chuckled. "What's the matter? Can't you find where it goes without help?" He snickered and motioned for the other man to follow.

Blade, beaming, stepped aside.

Cardew and the other man had taken several steps into the room before Cardew awoke to the danger. He saw the blood on Terza's chin and grabbed for his Browning. "Damn!"

Blade pounced. He kicked with his right leg, connecting on Cardew's left knee, and heard a distinct popping sound as Cardew screeched and dropped to the floor.

The second Leather Knight, a tall, lean black, went for the knife he wore in a sheath on his right hip.

Blade drove his right fist around and in, catching the black on the nose, crushing the cartilage and driving fragments into the Knight's forehead. He swung his left fist, boxing the Knight on the ear.

The stud started to drop.

Blade rammed his elbow into the man's jaw, then turned his attention to Cardew.

Still on the floor, wobbling on his right knee, Cardew was drawing his Browning.

Blade lashed out with his right foot, his toes smashing into Cardew's chin.

Cardew's head snapped backward. His teeth crunched together, and crimson spurted from his mouth.

"This is for last night!" Blade said, and hammered his left fist down on the right side of Cardew's face. Once. Twice.

Cardew groaned and sprawled onto the carpet.

Blade took the knife from the black and Cardew's Browning and hurried to the door.

The hallway was empty.

Blade closed the door behind him as he took a left. Reaching Rikki and Lex quickly was imperative. There was no telling how soon Terza and the others would be found.

Every moment counted.

The hulking Warrior reached a flight of stairs and hastily descended. Surprisingly, he reached the bottom level undetected. Maybe it wasn't so surprising, he told himself. Except for Terza, Cardew, and the guards, why would any of the Leather Knights be hanging around the library? From what he'd gathered, very few of them could even read. He cautiously opened the stairwell door and peeked outside.

The hallway leading to the holding chamber passed by the door. No one was in sight.

Blade took a right and ran down the hall. If all went well, he would reach—

A door up ahead opened and two Leather Knights, one man and one woman, emerged.

No!

"You!" the woman bellowed, clutching at the pistol she carried on her left side.

Blade shot her in the chest.

The woman twisted and fell to the floor.

Undaunted, the stud was trying to clear his revolver.

Blade planted a slug in the stud's head.

There was no use trying to conceal his movements now! Every Leather Knight in the building had heard the gunfire and would come running! Blade ran faster. He reached the door he'd used last night and flung it open.

Rikki and Lex were hanging from the far wall, still in chains. Both were gagged.

Blade raced across the dirt floor. He tore the gag from Rikki's mouth. "Where are the keys to your shackles?" he asked.

"The one called Cardew has them," Rikki replied.

Damn! Blade glared at the chains. Why hadn't he thought to search Cardew for the keys? After all, Cardew had unlocked *his* chains!

"We heard shooting," Rikki said.

"Hostile natives," Blade said, examining the antiquated chains.

"Take off," Rikki advised him. "You can come back and free us later."

"We're leaving here together," Blade stated.

"Without the keys?" Rikki asked.

"Who needs keys?" Blade tucked the Browning under his belt and handed the knife to Rikki. "Hold this."

"What do you have in mind?" Rikki inquired.

"This." Blade took hold of the chain attached to Rikki's right wrist. Removing the shackle encircing Rikki's wrist wasn't feasible; he could do it, but he might hurt Rikki in the bargain. No, his best bet was to concentrate on the link joining the chain to the shackle. He gripped the chain in his right hand and held the shackle with his left. "This might smart," he warned his companion.

Rikki's arm tensed. "Go for it."

Blade strained, exerting his herculean strength to its limit, pulling on the chain, his massive muscles bulging, his arms rippling with raw power.

Rikki had adopted the horse stance, striving to facilitate Blade's effort by staying as immobile as possible.

Blade was gritting his teeth, his neck pulsing, the veins protruding.

Lexine was watching the operation in wide-eyed astonishment.

Blade could feel the chain biting into his right hand. He igored the discomfort and heaved, thankful the chain was old and the links on the rusty side. If only they were weak enough! Sweat beaded his brow as he continued to apply pressure. Every muscle on his arms stood out in sharp relief. He closed his eyes, concentrating, channeling every iota of power into his brawny hands.

Rikki was striving to maintain his balance. Despite his horse stance, a normally immovable posture, Blade's awesome strength threatened to propel him from his feet.

Blade's sinews were at their utmost, his face a beet red, when the link affixed to the shackle on Rikki's right wrist snapped, parting with a loud crack.

Rikki relaxed. "You did it!" he said, elated.

Blade wiped his perspiring brow. "One down and three to go."

"You should rest a bit," Rikki advised.

"No time for that," Blade said. He moved sideways and applied himself to the shackle on Rikki's left wrist. This chain was more stubborn. The perspiration was pouring from his pores, his arms trembling from his exertion, when the connecting link finally broke.

Rikki rubbed his tender wrists, massaging the skin under the metal shackles. "Thank you," he said to his friend.

Blade nodded and crossed to Lex. He pulled the gag from her mouth.

"I don't believe it!" Lex declared. "How did you do it?"

"They don't make chains like they used to," Blade remarked.

Rikki joined them.

"You'll need to steady her arms," Blade directed Rikki. He looked at Lex. "If this hurts, say the word. If I'm not careful, I could tear your arms from their sockets."

"Don't worry none about me," Lex stated. "Just get me out of here!"

"I don't believe you two have been formally introduced," Rikki said as Blade took hold of the chain attached to Lexine's right wrist. "Blade, this is Lexine. Lex, this is Blade."

"Pleased to meet you," Lex mentioned.

Blade nodded and began applying himself to the chain.

Rikki gripped Lex's right wrist, adding support,

struggling to keep Lex's arm steady.

Lex grimaced as Blade started straining against the chain. The edge of the metal shackle bit into her flesh, drawing a thin line of blood. Even with Rikki holding her arm, she felt as if it really would be ripped from its socket any second.

Blade stared at the last link on the chain. He could see the rusted metal giving way and stretching. With a grunt, he wrenched the chain and was rewarded by a sharp, popping noise.

"Only one to do," Rikki said.

From off in the distance, from upstairs, came the din of upraised voices.

"They're after us!" Lex cried. "Hurry!"

Blade paused, gathering his energy. The clamor upstairs was growing louder. If the chain fastened to her left shackle was as sturdy as the others, it would require minutes to break.

He didn't have minutes to spare.

"Hold her left arm tightly," Blade said to Rikki, then he grinned at Lexine. "Close your eyes and count to three."

Lex did as he requested.

On the count of three, Blade tightened his arms and huge chest, took a deep breath, and savagely tugged on the chain.

Lex gasped as her left arm was jerked outward. Her left shoulder lanced with agony.

Blade uttered a growling sound and yanked his arms in opposite directions.

Lex groaned.

The link abruptly burst asunder, causing Blade to stumble backwards two feet.

"You're free!" Rikki said to Lex.

Lex leaned on the brick wall, holding her left arm pressed across her stomach. "Am I in one piece?" she asked, her eyes still shut.

Rikki rubbed her sore shoulder. "How bad is it?"

Lex opened her eyes and chuckled. "I'll live. We'd best get the hell out of here."

The approaching racket was much, much closer.

"Where are our weapons?" Blade queried Rikki.

"I don't know," Rikki replied.

"Then we'll have to make do with the Browning and the kife," Blade said. He glanced at Lex. "Which way?"

Lex scanned the chamber. "I'm not sure. I haven't been down here very often. One of these doors leads to an alley. But I can't remember which one."

"Lead the way," Blade instructed her.

"What if I pick the wrong door?" Lex responded.

"We'll have to take that risk," Blade said. "Let's go." He drew the Browning and motioned for them to precede him.

Lex headed for the nearest door, Rikki by her side with the knife held in his right hand.

Blade backed from the room, keeping his eyes on the door to the far hallway.

The Leather Knights were pounding down the hall.

Blade reached the door used by Lex and Rikki, turned, and darted into its dim interior.

Not a moment too soon.

Dozens of Leather Knights surged into the brick chamber. A great shout went up at the sight of the dangling chains.

"They're gone!" a man yelled above the rest. "But how?"

"We didn't pass 'em!" a woman bellowed. "They must have used one of the other doors!"

Immediately the Leather Knights divided up, some taking the first recessed door, others the second, and the smallest group the last door. In a minute, the chamber was vacant.

Far along the murky hallway and racing like the wind, Blade detected a swelling in the voices behind him as leather garbed bikers filled the narrow corridor.

Where did this lead?

Blade hoped the hall wasn't a dead end. He doubted the Leather Knights would bother to take them prisoner a second time, not after what he had done to Terza and Cardew. He locked his gaze on the shadowy forms of Rikki and Lex 30 feet ahead. If they could reach the alley Lex had mentioned, they might be able to hide in a nearby building. He wished he were outdoors instead of deep under the earth. A troubling sensation of claustrophobia enveloped him.

Spirit preserve him!

Blade glanced over his right shoulder, but couldn't perceive any movement to his rear.

Good.

They were losing the SOBs!

Blade faced front again and pounded after Rikki and Lex—

Rikki and Lex!

They were gone!

Blade stopped and peered into the gloom beyond. Had they outdistanced him? What could have happened?

"Blade!" came a subdued cry from Rikki. "Blade! Where are you?"

Blade twisted. Rikki's voice was coming from his left and behind him.

"Blade!" Rikki called once more.

"I'm here!" Blade yelled. "Where are you?"

"Did you miss the turn?" Rikki asked.

What turn? Blade realized he'd probably overlooked it when he had turned his head and scanned the tunnel! Now they were separated! "I must have missed it!" Blade confirmed.

"I'll keep talking," Rikki shouted. "Follow my voice."

Blade backtracked, running full speed, searching for a fork in the hallway.

"There's light ahead!" Rikki was saying. "It might be the alley!"

Blade reached a darkened bend in the hallway and discovered another branch bearing to the left. He was about to enter, but a sudden commotion rearward drew his attention.

Leather Knights were charging toward him from the direction of the brick chamber!

Blade hesitated. If he followed Rikki and Lex, the Leather Knights would chase after them to the alley and beyond. But if he stayed where he was, if he didn't take the left branch, Rikki and Lex could escape unmolested.

"There's one of 'em!" screamed a tall woman.

He'd been spotted! Blade turned his back on the left branch and took off, the Browning in his right hand.

With gleeful cries, the Leather Knights ran after the giant Warrior, ignoring the left branch in their eagerness to capture Blade.

As he raced deeper into the winding labyrinth below the library, with many of the tunnels and hallways bearing evidence of recent excavation, Blade wondered if he'd made the right move. Lit lanterns were few and far between. Often he would cover over a hundred yards in nearly complete darkness.

Some of the Leather Knights were carrying torches or lanterns, and the swiftest of them kept their quarry in sight as they doggedly pursued him, his fleeing form always visible, but barely, at the periphery of their flickering light.

Blade was beginning to think he might outdistance them. A grim smile touched his lips at the prospect. After he eluded them, he intended to scour the library for his weapns. Leaving St. Louis without his Bowies was unthinkable; the big knives were as much a part of him as his arms or legs.

The Leather Knights were determinedly sticking to his heels.

CAPITAL RUN

A lantern appeared directly ahead, suspended from a hook in the wall.

A junction, Blade thought.

But he was wrong.

Blade slowed, expecting to find a branch or fork in the hallway. Instead, he discovered a solid brick wall.

It was a dead end!

Furious, he whirled, facing the converging Leather Knights. They had him right where they wanted him! Outnumbered, with nowhere to turn! He raised the Browning and sighted on the nearest figure, now approximately 20 yards away.

Let them come!

They were about to learn why the Warriors were respected and feared far and wide.

Blade sighted and squeezed the trigger.

13

Hickok's amazement was plainly written all over his face. He gawked at the edifice before him, feeling as if he had stepped back through the pages of history to a prior era, to another day and age. He'd seen aged photographs of the White House in several of the books in the Family library, but the reality of actually observing the historically significant structure dwarfed the perceptions derived from viewing a picture. He could see six massive columns, formerly white but now faded and tarnished, in the middle of the building. On either side of the columns the walls were in fairly good shape, although all of the windows were broken or missing. A section of roof above the columns had caved in, littering the base of the columns with debris. "I'm in Washington, D.C.," the dazed gunman said to himself.

"Indeed you are," General Malenkov confirmed.

"But I can't be!" Hickok declared. "How'd I get here?"

"You were transported via helicopter," General Malenkov explained.

"All the way from St. Louis?" Hickok was boggled by the news. "That must be a thousand miles!"

"About eight hundred and sixty," General Malenkov stated. "You were unconscious the entire trip."

Hickok forced his mind to buckle down, to get a grip on his dilemma. How in the world was he going to get back to St. Louis? Eight hundred miles through hostile territory would be well-nigh unachievable. He needed time to think, to formulate a plan of action.

"Washington is the last place you expected to be, eh?" General Malenkov said.

Hickok nodded. "I don't understand. I'd heard Washington suffered a direct hit during World War III."

"It did," General Malenkov affirmed.

Hickok pointed at the White House. "Then what's that doin' there? A direct hit would've leveled the city."

General Malenkov leaned on the metal table. "A direct strike by a conventional thermonuclear device would destroy the city, yes. But we did not use a conventional device."

Hickok glanced at the general. "What did you use?"

"A neutron bomb."

Hickok's brow furrowed. "A neutron bomb?"

"Do you know what they are?" General Malenkov inquired.

"I think I read something about 'em years ago," Hickok said. "But I can't recollect what it was I read."

"I will enlighten you," General Malenkov offered. "To understand what happened, you must appreciate our strategy during the war. You see, Americans back then were really quite stupid. Only half of the population really believed a war was inevitable. The other half was either too absorbed in their own lives to even reflect on the likelihood of a conflict, or else they were gullible liberal fanatics who ignored our conquests worldwide and discounted all of our literature and policy statements clearly stating our goal of global domination. And even when the subject of a nuclear exchange was considered, the fools panicked. To them, a nuclear war was a worst-case scenario. Total annihilation. Radiation contaminating the environment for thousands of years to come." The general chuckled. "Of course, the American military leaders knew better, but they could not overcome the bias and ignorance of the media elite. The American leaders knew we entertained no intention of destroying the country. Why should we? Soviet leaders knew how rich this land is in natural resources. At a time when we were barely able to feed our own people, why would we ruin the breadbasket of the Western Hemisphere? Our military leaders did use typical thermonuclear devices on carefully selected targets, but where possible we used other weapons like the neutron bomb."

"So what's a neutron bomb?" Hickok queried.

"A neutron bomb is a lot like an ordinary H-bomb, but it is not as destructive. It doesn't have the same explosive power and produces far less fallout. Some years before the war, there was a controversy in America over the deployment of the neutron bomb in Europe. The idiotic press campaigned against the idea. Their inconsistency was incredible. They preferred to use the terribly destructive hydrogen warheads instead of the smaller, cleaner neutron variety." General Malenkov paused. "I have diligently studied the prewar era, and I was constantly shocked by the ignorance displayed by the predominantly liberal media in America. I think their unrestrained freedom gave them an illusion of power. They believed they knew how the country should be run better than the officials elected to run it. In the U.S.S.R.," he boasted, "we had no such problem."

"So Washington, D.C., is still standin'," Hickok said, gazing at the White House.

"We knew how important this city was to the American public," General Malenkov revealed. "What a monumental psychological victory to occupy the capital of our hated enemy! The neutron bomb inflicted damage to many of the buildings, but otherwise Washington emerged from the war much as it was before our invasion began." He nodded toward the White House. "No one is permited to live there now. It stands as a symbol of American decadence and capitalistic corruption. This room we are in is located in our North American Headquarters. It was constructed on the south lawn of the White House, both as a symbol of our victory and a reminder to the American people of our superiority."

"Don't you Russians believe in modesty?" Hickok cracked.

General Malenkov frowned. "What do we have to be modest about? We won, didn't we?"

"Did you?" Hickok countered.

"What do you mean?" General Malenkov demanded.

"I've been doin' some thinkin'," Hickok said. "And some things don't add up. For instance, why didn't you take over the whole country? Where'd you stop— at the Mississippi? How much of the country do you control anyway?"

General Malenkov straightened. "You ask too many questions, Hickok. I can't answer them all now. Why don't you rest, and we will continue our conversation later?"

"Whatever you say," Hickok stated, and stared out the window.

General Malenkov took a step toward the door, positioned at the opposite end of the room from the window.

"Pardon me, my general," Lieutenant Voroshilov made bold to speak, resorting to Russian so the fool in the buckskins could not understand.

General Malenkov stopped. "What is it?" he responded in kind.

Lieutenant Voroshilov indicated Hickok with a nod of his head. "I don't trust him," he said. "Why don't we subject the idiot to proper interrogation and be done with this nonsense? Why do you treat him so politely? You know he must be an enemy of the people?"

"Of course I know it," General Malenkov said with a trace of annoyance, irritated his subordinate would presume to challenge his judgment.

"Then why not inject him with our serum?" Lieutenant Voroshilov suggested. "Or hand him over to the Committee for State Security? They will make him tell the truth."

"Certainly they would," General Malenkov agreed, "but he might not survive the interrogation. The KGB are not gentle in their work." He sighed and draped his right arm over Voroshilov's shoulders. "My dear Nikolai," he said paternally, "how do you expect to advance in rank if you will not exercise the discretion required of a senior-grade officer? Yes, I could have permitted the KGB to take him. But what if he didn't survive their cross-examination? Where would that leave us? I receive the impression he is very strong, very disciplined. He would undoubtedly resist our efforts, force our interrogators to apply harsher measures. Many prisoners have died before they could be compelled to tell all they know. Even the serum has drawbacks. It is not infallible, and has adverse side effects. You say I am treating him politely. Hasn't it occurred to you there is a reason for this? I am judging the man, evaluating his character. By pretending to be friendly, I might win his confidence. I could learn his weaknesses. He might unwittingly reveal an exploitable factor we can use to our advantage. Didn't you see the look on his face when he mentioned the name of his vehicle? He didn't intend to tell us, but it slipped out. Do you comprehend?"

Lieutenant Voroshilov nodded sheepishly.

"I can turn him over to the KGB at any time," General Malenkov went on. "What's the rush? This is a most extraordinary case. I recognized its importance the moment I saw the report on this SEAL. Why do you think I took personal charge of the case? Why did I order this man to be brought here? We must proceed slowly. This calls for finesse, not brute force." He thoughtfully stared at the tiled floor. "Our own vehicles are in disrepair. We don't have enough spare parts to go around. Our helicopter fleet has been greatly reduced, and we dare not use our jets because they are too old and unreliable. Yet this SEAL appears to be in perfect shape. We must learn more about it and the people who own it. Do they have any more? Where did it really come from? I don't believe Hickok's story for a second. We must be patient, lieutenant. Haste only breeds incompetence."

Unnoticed by the picture window, Hickok surreptitiously peered at his captors. The general and the lieutenant were having a heart-to-heart about something, and they both had their backs to him. The third soldier, the one with the pistol, had relaxed his guard and was listening to the two officers.

This might be his big chance!

The wooden stand with his Pythons was to the left of the officers. The armed soldier was to their right.

How could he get to his Colts without being shot?

Hickok scanned the room. To his right was the row of medical equipment. He spotted a shelf near the edge of the window. On the shelf were shiny instruments: a forked object, one with a small circular mirror on its tip, a metal disk, and others. One of them appeared to be a thin knife.

The general and the lieutenant were talking away.

Hickok casually ambled toward the shelf, his hands clasped in front of him, his back to the room, feigning interest in the White House.

The Russians didn't seem to notice.

Hickok reached the end of the window and calmly glanced behind him, a smile on his lips.

General Malenkov and Lieutenant Voroshilov were still jabbering. The third soldier idly glanced at the gunman, then back at the officers.

Hickok nonchalantly leaned his right hand on the shelf while gazing out the window. Slowly, expecting to be challenged at any moment, he inched his fingers to the handle of the silver knife. He covered the handle with his palm, then slowly closed his hand around the knife.

Malenkov was expounding on some subject to Voroshilov.

Hickok mentally counted to ten, and then eased his right hand from the shelf and lowered it by his side.

None of the Russians had noticed.

Hickok held the knife close to his leg.

"I must leave now," General Malenkov said in English to the gunman. "I will return in an hour and escort you to the commissary."

"The what?" Hickok asked.

"The commissary," General Malenkov said. "You will be able to eat."

"Thanks," Hickok stated. "I'm so hungry I could eat a horse."

"I will treat you to some borscht," General Malenkov commented. "It's a traditional Russian dish."

"What's in it?"

The general licked his lips. "It's delicious. Borscht contains beets and sour cream."

"I can hardly wait," Hickok said deadpan.

General Malenkov smiled. "See you in an hour." He walked to the door with Lieutenant Voroshilov in tow. At the door he halted and looked at the soldier with the pistol. "If he tries to escape," the general ordered in Russian, "shoot him in the groin. I want him alive."

The soldier nodded and saluted.

Hickok waved as the general and the lieutenant left

the room. He grinned at the soldier and pointed at the White House. "They sure don't make 'em like that anymore, do they?"

The soldier didn't respond. He was a stocky man with dark hair and a square chin. The pistol was held steady in his right hand, aimed at the gunman.

"Don't you savvy English?" Hickok inquired.

The soldier remained immobile.

"What's the matter? Can't you palaver without permission?" Hickok asked.

The soldier's face creased in perplexity.

"So you can speak English," Hickok said.

"Please," the soldier remarked, "what is 'palaver'?"

"It means to shoot the breeze," Hickok explained. "Sling the bull. You know. Idle chitchat."

The soldier seemed even more confused. "I know English, yes. But I do not know many of the words you use."

Hickok took a few steps toward the soldier, acting innocent. He grinned. "That's because I'm partial to Old West lingo I picked up in books in our library."

"Does everyone where you are from talk like you do?" the soldier asked.

"Nope," Hickok acknowledged. "I'm the only one."

"Most strange," the soldier commented.

Hickok nodded in agreement and moved several feet closer to the soldier. "That's what my friends say too."

"Then why do you do it?" the soldier queried.

"I reckon my momma must of dropped me on my noggin when I was six months old," Hickok said. He took two more steps nearer to the soldier.

"You will stay where you are," the guard warned.

Hickok shrugged. "Whatever you say, pard. But I've got a question for you."

"A question?"

"Yeah. Do you mind if I ask it?" Hickok inquired.

"What is your question?" the soldier wanted to know.

"I don't reckon there's any chance of you letting me walk out that door, is there?" Hickok ventured to request.

The soldier laughed. "You are not serious, yes?"

"Deadly serious," Hickok gravely informed him.

The soldier shook his head. "Nyet. I can not allow you to leave this room."

"What would you do if I tried?" Hickok asked.

"I would shoot you," the soldier soberly responded.

Hickok sighed. "And I don't suppose there's nothin' I could say or do that would change your mind?"

"I will shoot you," the soldier reiterated.

"Well, you can't say I didn't try," Hickok said. He half turned, looking at the White House. "I can always spend my time counting the cracks in the walls."

The soldier shifted his attention to the decaying structure. "A most fitting fate for the decadent warmongers," he stated, quoting from a course he'd taken in Imperialist Practices and Fallacies.

"Speaking of fate," Hickok said slowly. He suddenly whipped his lean body around, his right hand flashing up and out.

The silver knife streaked across the intervening space and sliced into the soldier's right eye. He shrieked and clutched at the hilt, but the blood spurting from his ravaged eyeball made the handle too slippery to clasp. His trigger finger tightened on the trigger of his pistol, but before he could pull it he started to tremble uncontrollably. Spasms racked his body. His facial muscles quivered as he arched his back and staggered into the metal table.

Hickok knew the man was in his death throes.

The soldier's fingers involuntarily relaxed,

straightening, and the pistol dropped to the floor. He gasped and sprawled onto the table, on his stomach, blood dribbling from the corners of his mouth, his nostrils, and his punctured eye. His good eye locked on the gunman, and with a whining wheeze he expired.

Hickok walked to the wooden stand and retrieved his Pythons. He stared at the gleaming pearl-handled Colts, feeling complete again. What had they done with his Henry? he wondered. He hoped they'd overlooked it in the dark and it was still in the woods near the SEAL.

The SEAL.

How the blazes was he going to return to St. Louis? He needed to come up with one humdinger of an idea.

Voices, speaking in Russian, came through the closed wooden door.

It was time to hit the road.

Hickok quickly checked the pythons, and it was well he did. Someone had unloaded them while he was unconscious. He slipped the necessary cartridges from his gunbelt and reloaded both Colts.

Now let them try and stop him!

The gunman eased to the door and cautiously opened it. He found an amply lit corridor with brown floor tiles and white walls.

None of the varmints were in sight.

Hickok took a deep breath and stepped out of the medical room. He closed the door behind him and hurried to the left, searching for a place of concealment, somewhere he could get his bearings.

A door directly ahead abruptly opened and a tall woman in a white smock emerged.

Blast!

The woman spotted the gunman, her face registering utter bewilderment. She recovered and said something in Russian.

Hickok bounded forward.

The woman was opening her mouth to scream when the gunman slammed the barrel of his right Colt across her jaw.

The woman stumbled backard, bumping into the wall.

Hickok slugged her again for good measure.

She sagged to the floor in a disjointed heap.

Hickok ran now, knowing he had to get out of the building before the alarm was given. He hated being cooped up inside. Once outdoors, the odds of eluding his captors were infinitely better. He reached a fork in the corridor and bore to the left again. He was thankful he was on the ground floor; at least he wouldn't need to contend with finding the right stairs.

Two men, both in military uniforms, one armed with a holstered pistol, another with a machine gun— an AK-47, if Hickok remembered the gun manuals in the Family library correctly—appeared at the end of the corridor. They reacted to the gunman's presence instantly, the one with the pistol grabbing for his holster and the other soldier sweeping his AK-47 up.

Hickok was 30 feet from them. He never broke his stride as he leveled the Colts and fired, both Pythons booming simultaneously.

The two soldiers each took a slug between the eyes. The one with the pistol simply fell forward, but the trooper with the AK-47 tottered backwards, crashed into the left-hand wall, and dropped.

Hickok slowed as he neared the soldiers. He holstered the Colts and leaned over the soldier with the AK-47. "I need this more than you," he commented, scooping the gun into his arms and continuing to the end of the hallway.

Bingo!

Wide glass doors were on the other side of a spacious reception area. A woman at an oaken desk was frantically punching buttons on an instrument of some kind.

Hickok was abreast of her desk before he recalled the name of the contraption she was using: a telephone. They had used them before the Big Blast for communications purposes.

The woman started yelling into the receiver.

Hickok gripped the barrel of the AK-47 and swung it like a club, striking the receptionist on the left side of her head.

She slid from her chair to the floor, the telephone plopping alongside her.

Move!

Hickok ran to the glass doors. He paused, confused. The dang things didn't have any doorknobs! How was he supposed to—

The doors unexpectedly parted with a pronounced hiss.

What the—

Hickok raced outside. Never look a gift horse in the mouth! he always said. He scanned the scenery before him. From the position of the sun, he knew he was heading due south. In front, a park with trees and grass and couples strolling arm-in-arm and kids playing with puppies. To the right, a parking lot filled with vehicles. To the left, a sidewalk and a hedgerow.

Which way?

Hickok bore to the left, making for the hedge. He could hide and take a breather while he—

Four soldiers pounded into view, coming his way, jogging around the hedgerow on the sidewalk.

Someone in the park had seen the gunman and was shouting at the top of his lungs.

In the parking lot, three troopers hopped from a jeep and raced toward him.

Behind him, the glass doors hissed open, disgorging three more soldiers in hot pursuit.

Hickok crouched and raised the AK-47.

So much for subterfuge!

14

The blast of the Browning was practically deafening in the narrow confines of the hallway.

The leading Leather Knight toppled forward, shot through the chest.

Blade aimed at a second target, his finger tightening on the trigger.

A hard object rammed into the small of the Warrior's back.

"Drop it!" a stern voice commanded. "Or you can kiss your navel good-bye!"

Blade hesitated. How had one of them managed to get behind him?

"I ain't kidding, sucker!" snapped the speaker, a woman by the sound of her voice. "Drop it or I'll blow you away for what you did to Terza!"

Blade released the Browning and it clattered to the ground.

The onrushing Leather Knights had slowed and were cautiously advancing toward the prisoner, their weapons trained and cocked.

"Turn around, you son of a bitch!" ordered the woman behind the Warrior.

Blade turned, his hands held over his head.

She was a heavyset blonde with a scowl on her face. "The name's Erika, prick! And I'm gonna make sure you never forget it!"

"With a face like yours," Blade told her, "I doubt I ever will."

Erika's fleshy features reddened. "I'm gonna enjoy wasting you!" She held a Ruger Security-Six revolver in her left hand.

Blade studied the "dead end." The central portion of the wall was actually a concealed door. Beyond Erika's squat form was a spacious chamber basking in the light from ten lanterns. Other Knights were in the chamber, standing, staring at the doorway.

Erika glanced at the mob in the corridor. "You did a good job. We'll take him now." She paused. "What about the other two? Lex and her lover boy?"

"We didn't see them," admitted a stud.

"Go look for them," Erika said. "Search every nook and cranny. We want them found! They have to pay for what they did!"

The Leather Knights wheeled and ran down the hall. Two of them stopped and knelt alongside the man Blade had shot.

Erika poked Blade in the ribs with the Ruger Security-Six. "One false move and you're history!" she warned. She backed through the doorway, beckoning with the revolver for him to follow.

Blade entered the chamber, his arms in the air.

There were 11 Leather Knights in the room. Like the other sections displaying evidence of recent construction, this chamber was built of brick and the floor was mere dirt. Unlike the holding chamber with the balcony, this one had a large pit in the middle of the room. The Leather Knights ringed the pit, all of them armed. Two of them stood ten feet from the door, and they riveted baleful glares on the Warrior as he appeared.

"So happy you could join us," said Terza dryly. She wore her black leather jacket and pants. Her Llama Super Comanche V's were belted around her waist. "We're havin' a little party and you're the guest of honor." She seemed to experience difficulty in speaking, and her jaw was slightly swollen. Her pale blue eyes glittered as she gazed at Blade.

Next to her, Cardew's face reflected his sheer hatred. His right cheek was puffy and his right eye a narrow slit covered by a discolored, distended eyelid. Both of his lips were split and twice their normal size. A wooden splint had been applied to his left knee, and he had improvised a wooden crutch to support himself.

"I didn't expect to see you up and around so soon," Blade said to the stud. "I guess you have more guts than I gave you credit for. Too bad they're all between your ears."

Cardew went livid.

Terza motioned for the Warrior to come closer.

Blade lowered his arms and advanced to within a foot of the Leather Knight leader.

"You're a fine one to talk about Cardew," Terza said. "You aren't exactly the brightest man I ever met." She snickered. "But then, what else can you expect from a lousy man?"

"Not much," Erika chimed in.

Terza sneered at Blade. "You blew it, handsome. You had your big chance and you plain blew it." She lowered her voice so only Blade, Cardew, and Erika could overhear her remarks. "I wanted you, tiger. And like I told you before, I don't get the hots for a man all that often. Who knows? If you'd been any good, I might have spared your ass. But as it is—"

Blade snickered. "I don't think I missed much."

Terza's right hand gripped her right Comanche.

"You're the vainest woman I've ever met," Blade went on. "You think all you have to do is snap your fingers and any man in the world will do anything for the . . . honor . . . of bedding you." He paused. "You're wrong, Terza. You don't have the right to force a man to have sex with you. Sex isn't some mechanical function we perform for fleeting physical gratification. Sex should be an expression of our deepest love, our tenderest feelings. You denigrate it to an animalistic level. To you, sex is on the same par with eating or sleeping or any other purely physical sensation. Why don't you try exalting sex for once? Why don't you find someone to love, and express your love as meaningfully sexually as you know how. You never know," he concluded. "You might learn something."

"You dare talk to me like this?" Terza demanded.

"I'll talk to you any way I please," Blade countered. "I'm not one of your lackeys, your cowardly studs."

Cardew made a growling noise.

Blade glanced at Cardew's pulverized face. "What's the matter with you? Does the truth hurt? When was the last time the men around here had the balls to stand up to the women? Why do you let them push you around, to control your lives the way they do? Men and women should be equal partners in adjusting to life's responsibilities. Neither gender has the right to subjugate the other." He raised his voice so the others in the chamber could hear. "When are the Leather Knight men going to reclaim their proper place as equals with the women? When are the men going to stand on their own two feet and refuse to be little better than slaves? When will the men—"

Terza abruptly lunged upward, slapping Blade across the mouth. "Shut up! That's enough out of you! Who the hell do you think you are, coming in here and telling us how to live our lives? We've lived this way for a hundred years—"

"Does that make it right?" Blade interrupted.

"Yes!" Terza replied. "It's no worse than the way it was before the war."

"Before the war?"

"I'm not all *that* stupid," Terza declared angrily. "I can read some, and I know how it was before the war. The men ran everything. The government they had, all the businesses, the military, everything. Oh, there were a few women at the top, but they were far outnumbered by the men. The men controlled things, but they pretended the women had an equal say. The damn hypocrites! At least we're honest about it!"

"Does that make it right?" Blade reiterated.

Terza was obviously flustered. She'd been taken off guard by Blade's unexpected behavior. She'd expected him to either beg for his life or else clam up and take what was coming as stoically as possible. She considered him to be the "macho" type, the "strong, silent type," the kind who habitually lorded it over women. She'd encountered outsiders before, and the men were all pretty much the same. The last reaction she'd anticipated was a verbal assault on her morals.

Blade sensed her emotional upheaval and determined to press his advantage. "Terza, we don't need to be enemies. We can be friends instead. My people would welcome a treaty with yours. We could work together, helping you to rebuild your city and oppose the Reds. I came here on a peaceful mission. I'd like to leave in peace."

"Peace!" Terza snorted. "Where is there peace in this world? You tell me that, Mister High-and-Mighty! If you want to survive in this rotten world, you've got to be tough. It's survival of the fittest." She shook her head. "Do you think we'd be dumb enough to trust you? For all we know, your people are waiting for the chance to jump us, to attack St. Louis the moment we let down our guard. But I've got news for you! The Leather Knights will never be beaten. Not even the Reds have beaten us! Look around you. Why do you think we've gone to all the trouble to build all these new tunnels and rooms under the library? And we've also done it under some of the other buildings. Because we know the Reds are gonna come after us someday, and we're gonna be ready for 'em! These tunnels will be the last retreat for those who can't make it out of the city. We have food stockpiled and plenty of guns and ammo. We've thought of everything!" she boasted.

"Except how the women and men can live in harmony," Blade responded.

"Who the hell cares about that?" Terza gruffly demanded.

"The men do," Blade said. "And I bet some of the women as well. I understand Lex was leaving the Leather Knights because she doesn't agree with the way you run things. Do you think she's the only one?"

"No one leaves the Leather Knights," Terza said. "And as for the men, they'll do what the hell we tell them, when we tell them, or they'll get what you're gonna get."

Blade scanned the chamber, noting the pensive, troubled faces of the men. He knew he'd touched a raw nerve. "With an attitude like yours," he told Terza, "it's only a question of time before the women have a full-scale rebellion on their hands. It's inevitable. Sooner or later, the men will have had enough, they'll have taken all they will take. And what will happen? You'll have a bloody civil war on your hands, the studs against the sisters. After it's over, one side or the other will assume control. What if the men win?"

"They never will!" Terza vowed.

"What if neither side wins?" Blade continued. "What if both sides are so depleted there aren't enough remaining to rule St. Louis? And all because the women believe they're better than the men. What a waste!"

"We *are* better than the men!" Terza stated irritably. She saw the expressions on the six men in the room and realized the giant stranger was right: the studs did resent the sisters' domination.

"Women aren't better than men," Blade was saying. "And men aren't better than women. They're just different from one another. The secret is to recognize the differences and complement each other, whether in a marriage or in society as a whole."

"This bozo is so full of bullshit it's coming out of his ears," Erika interrupted.

Cardew took a tentative step toward Blade. He tried to speak, but couldn't form the worlds. At last, after licking his busted lips, he managed to croak a question. "Do you . . . believe . . . all that stuff?"

"Of course," Blade confirmed.

"Enough of this!" Terza barked. "You're just stallin'! We aren't here to shoot the shit!"

"Let's get down to cases!" Erika said eagerly.

"Do you have any idea where you are?" Terza asked.

"How should I?" Blade replied.

"This is a special room," Terza mentioned. "We built it for just one reason."

Blade stared at the gaping pit. The sight of it stirred memories of the last pit he'd seen, the one he'd been tossed into by a madman on the run to Denver, Colorado. He repressed an impulse to shudder.

"This hole is real unique," Terza explained. "It connects to the city's sewers. Ever seen a sewer?"

Blade shook his head.

"The sewers don't get used much anymore," Terza said. "Before the war, they pumped all the shit and the piss and the garbage through 'em. There's a lot of passages under the city, in all different shapes and sizes. Some of the sewer tunnels are real big, so big a person can walk in 'em. Others are so small even the rats can't use 'em. Do you know what else is down there, besides the rats?"

Blade simply stared at her.

Terza averted his gaze, facing the pit. "We don't know what caused them, but there are a lot of . . . things . . . in the sewers. Maybe it was the radiation in the water, or something was pumped into the sewer system. We found some old barrels once in one of the tunnels, and some chemical gook had seeped out of 'em. Whatever the reason, there are a lot of creepy, crawly things down there."

"So?" Blade finally said.

"So this hole leads to the sewers where the things live. One of the things . . ." she grinned, "is called Grotto. You have to see it to believe it."

"Grotto craves flesh," Erika commented, grinning wickedly.

"And Grotto hasn't eaten for a while," Terza declared. "Three guesses who its next meal is gonna be."

Blade frowned, calculating the odds of escaping from the chamber. There weren't any. The Leather Knights would gun him down before he traveled three feet.

Terza glanced at the Warrior. "Any last words?"

"I feel sorry for you," Blade said.

"Sorry for me?" Terza retorted in disbelief. "*You're* the one who's gonna be mutant bait, dimwit!"

"You may succeed in killing me," Blade said, "but in doing so you'll destroy yourselves."

"What are you babbling about?" Terza demanded.

"I have friends," Blade told her. "They'll come after me. One of them, in particular, won't rest until he finds out what happened to me. And when he does find out, one way or another he'll guarantee the Leather Knights are wiped out."

"Should we tremble now or later?" Erika joked.

Blade shrugged. "I knew you wouldn't believe me."

"What is this joker?" Terza queried. "Some kind of superman?"

"No," Blade said. "He's not a superman. But he's the most lethal person I know. You might say he's sort of a living leathal weapon."

"Oh! I'm scared!" Erika said in mock panic, and

laughed.

"Suit yourself," Blade said.

Terza walked to the edge of the pit. "Let's get this over with! Summon Grotto."

One of the Knights on the other side of the pit, a tall, bearded stud, sank to his knees. He grasped a board lying near the edge and raised it over his head.

"I can hardly wait!" Erika said, elated.

The stud proceeded to slam the flat board against the side of the pit, again and again, filling the chamber with a regular cadence of thuds.

Blade inched nearer to the hole, examining it. The sides were 20 feet deep and solid earth. The floor was littered with white bones: thigh bones, ribs, skulls, and more, all distinctly human.

Cardew was staring thoughtfully at Blade. "Say," he was able to croak, "I never did get your name."

"It's Blade," the Warrior said.

"Too bad we couldn't have met under different circumstances," Cardew stated wistfully.

Blade looked at the Knight, surprised. Cardew seemed to be sincere. Maybe he wasn't a total degenerate after all.

The bearded stud maintained his constant pounding.

"It won't be long!" Erika cried.

Terza glanced at Blade. "What a waste."

"I'm not dead yet," Blade reminded her.

"You will be," Terza said.

"Don't I receive a fighting chance?" Blade asked her.

"A fighting chance?"

"Yeah. Like my Bowies."

Terza laughed. "Are you wacko? Do you really expect me to hand your knives back to you? No way, turkey. They're upstairs. I may take one of them for myself after this is over."

"No weapons then?" Blade inquired, knowing how

she would respond.

"No weapons," Terza affirmed. "Just you and Grotto. You two should become real cozy down there."

The bearded stud was beginning to tire. His pounding was losing some of its force.

"Where the hell is it?" Erika snapped.

"It takes a while sometimes," Terza said. "You know that."

A loud hissing suddenly emanated from the pit.

"Grotto!" Erika cried happily.

They all craned their necks for a good view of the bottom of the pit.

For the first time, Blade noticed a subterranean entrance to the pit. Located on the north side, it was a black hole about ten feet in height and eight feet wide.

The Leather Knights were collectively watching that hole.

The hissing had ceased.

"We've been doing this for near thirty years," Terza said to Blade. "Not in this room, because it wasn't built at the time, but in the sewers. Some of the Knights had seen Grotto prowling the sewers, and someone once had the bright idea of feedin' outsiders to it. Grotto loves fresh meat," Terza said, grinning.

"What do you have against outsiders?" Blade asked.

"We don't need any more people in St. Louis," Terza answered. "We already have about as many as the Knights can handle. Besides, outsiders always want to change things. They're just like you. Know-it-all bastards who stick their noses in where they don't belong! So when we were constructing our underground retreat, we built this hidden room next to one of the sewer tunnels. Now we can call Grotto directly from here."

"How convenient," Blade said. "A walk-in

restaurant for a mutant."

"What's a restaurant?" Terza inquired.

"A place where you can eat fine food," Blade replied. "They had a lot of them before the war."

"Then that's what this is," Terza said. "Grotto's restaurant."

Another stud had taken over the pounding chores, but there was still no sign of the mysterious monster.

"Maybe it doesn't like your service," Blade quipped. "Do you supply napkins and tableware?"

"I don't know what you're talkin' about," Terza said. "Grotto will show up. Sometimes it takes a while, but it always shows up."

"Once it took most of the day," Erika commented. "Damn! I hope it doesn't take that long this time!"

"I can wait," Blade informed them.

Terza laughed lightly. "I bet you can."

15

"What do you think happened to him?" Lex asked.

"I don't know," Rikki-Tikki-Tavi responded.

The Warrior was concerned for the safety of his friend. He'd heard the hubbub caused by the Leather Knights in the adjacent hallway, and it was easy to figure out Blade's selfless sacrifice in diverting the Knights away from the passage leading to the alley.

"What are we going to do?" Lex questioned him.

"Wait," Rikki told her.

"For what?"

"Until Blade returns," Rikki said.

"What if he doesn't?"

"Then we go looking for him," Rikki stated.

They were crouched along the hallway wall not ten feet from the exit to the alley. The Knights hadn't bothered to install a door at the end of the hallway. The opening permitted brilliant sunlight to flood the hall for over 20 yards.

Lex glanced at the exit: so inviting, so tempting, so close! One quick dash and she would gain her freedom. She looked at the lean man beside her, his face in profile as he gazed down the hallway hoping to see the big one called Blade. She remembered the pained look on his face when Terza had been using her for target practice. Her feminine intuition sensed he cared, and she found herself delighted at the prospect. "You're really worried about him, aren't you?" she asked.

Rikki nodded.

"How long have you know him?"

"All of my life," Rikki stated. "He's only a year older than I am. We were childhood friends and we grew to manhood together. We even selected the same path."

"The same path?" Lex repeated.

"Yes. The path of the Warrior," Rikki said. "Blade is the head of the Warriors. I will not depart St. Louis without him."

Lex could detect the undisguised affection in Rikki's tone. "Are there many of you Warriors?" she asked, keeping her voice low.

"Fifteen," Rikki disclosed.

"Why are you called Warriors?"

Rikki glanced at her. "My people are known as the Family. We live in a walled compound far away. The man responsible for constructing the compound and gathering the subsequent survivors of the war together knew they would require protection. He knew civilization would crumble after World War III. He predicted society would revert to primitive levels, and he was right. To safeguard the Family from the scavengers, the marauding bands of killers, and mutates, and others, he formed a special corps of fighters and designated them as the Warriors. For over one hundred years the Warriors have defended the Family from all attackers. We take a solemn oath, and any one of us would give our life in the performance of our duty."

"Why did you want to be a Warrior?" Lex asked.

"It is my nature," Rikki responded simply.

"I don't understand."

"No two individuals are alike," Rikki elaborated. "No two of us have the same personality, the same characteristics, or the same abilities. Our natures are essentially different. My Family is an excellent example. Some of us prefer to be Tillers of the soil.

Others choose to be Weavers, or Healers, or Empaths, or Blacksmiths. Each according to his or her nature. I wanted to become a Warrior because it was inherent in my personality. The Family Elders don't force anyone into a vocation against his or her will. They encourage each of us to find our particular calling and devote our talents to it." He paused. "It wasn't always this way. I've read some history books detailing life before the Big Blast—"

"The Big Blast?"

"That's what the Family calls World War III," Rikki explained. "Before the war, society tried to mold every individual into a set pattern. Every aspect of their lives was strictly regulated by countless laws. Amazingly, the people back then considered themselves to be free. The irony is, it took a nuclear war to actually liberate them."

"You don't sound like you would have been too happy back then," Lex remarked.

"I wouldn't have been," Rikki admitted. "I would have resented every intrusion on my freedom. Why, they even passed laws making it illegal to carry a weapon in public! Can you imagine that?"

"Why would they do such a thing?"

"Because they wanted the populace as docile as cattle," Rikki said bitterly. "Their society was overrun by criminals and degenerates, but the so-called leaders wouldn't allow the people to carry weapons to defend themselves. The leaders claimed it would promote vigilantism."

"What's that?"

"That's where the average person stands up to someone who is threatening them in some way."

"And the leaders didn't want that?" Lex asked, perplexed.

"Not according to my teacher, Plato," Rikki said. "You see, such an attitude promotes independence. If people can supply their own needs and defend themselves from the violent defectives, then they don't have any need for anyone else to tell them how to live, what they should wear and eat and think. No, the leaders were afraid of vigilantism. They were frightened by self-reliant individualism. So they stifled intiative and suppressed creativity." He frowned. "No, I would never have fit in back then. Don't get me wrong. I'm not anti-social by any standard. I believe in peaceful relations with all men and women. But a lot of degenerates don't feel the same way. They'd slit your throat as soon as look at you." He smiled at her. "And I would never permit that."

Lex recognized the compliment. "You've given this a lot of thought," she noted.

"What use is a mind if you don't use it?" Rikki rejoined.

"What's it like?" Lex inquired. "This place you're from."

Rikki sighed. "You'd enjoy it. We all believe in the ideal of loving our neighbor and serving the Spirit. We may argue about various issues, but overall our relations are harmonious. Far better than anything I've seen anywhere else."

"It sounds like a dream come true," Lex said.

"Would you like to go there?" Rikki asked her.

Lex brightened. "Would they let me come?"

"They would welcome you with open arms," Rikki confirmed. "Especially if you had a sponsor in the Family."

"What's a sponsor?"

"Someone in the Family who vouches for your integrity."

"Who—" Lex began.

"I would," Rikki said quickly.

"You'd do that for me?"

Rikki nodded and stared down the hallway.

Now the exit to the alley was even more appealing.

Lex wanted to flee the library, the leave St. Louis far behind. Rikki's home seemed too good to be true. She wanted to live to find out for herself. "What's this place where you're from called?"

"The Home."

"The Home?" Lex giggled. "Where else would the Family live, right?"

Rikki grinned.

"You must have a lot of friends there," Lex stated.

"Many close friends," Rikki affirmed.

"Tell me about them," she urged him.

"Most of my closest friends are Warriors like myself," Rikki said. "You'll meet them. There's Geronimo, who took his name after an Indian chief of long, long ago. One of them is named Hickok, the Family's supreme gunfighter."

"Is he better with guns than you?" Lex interjected.

"Much better," Rikki acknowledged. "His expertise with guns, particularly handguns, is sensational. We have a Warrior called Yama, and he's good with every weapon. Teucer specializes in the bow. Others excel with different weapons."

"What are you best with?"

"A katana," Rikki said. "My instructors felt I was the best martial artist in the family. Consequently, I qualified to possess the katana."

"What's a martial artist?"

Rikki stared at her. "Someone skilled in hand-to-hand combat and with Oriental weaponry."

"What's hand-to-hand combat? Punching somebody's lights out?"

Rikki chuckled. "My answer was rather simplistic. A martial artist is adept in the science of unarmed and armed combat. It's more than just knowing how to punch somebody's lights out. It's a way of life, a discipline in which you become the ultimate master of yourself. A perfected martial artist is at one with his Maker, with the universe, and with himself.

Sublime control enables you to live without fear. You achieve an inner peace, and this is reflected in your relations with others."

"This is all a little over my head," Lex admitted.

"I can teach you if you want," Rikki offered.

Their eyes met, and a mutual tenderness was silently shared.

"You never did tell me," Lex said after a bit, "why you picked such a strange name?"

"It was the logical choice," Rikki said. "The Founder of our Home encouraged all of his followers to learn from the mistakes humankind had perpetuated in the past. He was afraid we would lose sight of the stupidity behind the war. So he started the Naming at age sixteen. All Family members, when they turn sixteen, are allowed to pick any name they want from any of the books in our vast library. This way, the Founder hoped, we wouldn't forget our roots. At first, they used only the history books. But now any book is okay. I took my name from a story concerning an animal known as a mongoose."

"A mongoose?"

"Small animals," Rikki said. "They were used in a country called India to protect their families from deadly snakes known as cobras."

"So that's why you took the name!"

"Yes. It fits my chosen profession," Rikki stated.

They lapsed into a short silence.

"What about you?" Rikki finally asked. "I've told you a lot about myself. Tell me something about your life."

Lex shrugged, her green eyes betraying a hint of sadness. "What's to tell? I was raised by my mom and dad in the northwest part of the city. When I was fifteen, one of the sisters nominated me to become a Knight. I was thrilled. I thought it was the biggest honor there was."

"Now you don't think so?"

"No!" Lex said, her voice hardening. "They fed me all that garbage about women being superior to men when I was young, and I believed it. I ran roughshod over the studs like all of the other sisters. But something happened."

"What?"

"The older I got," Lex said bitterly, "the more I realized how sick the situation was. I mean, here we have all of these women bossing the men around like the males are the scum of the earth. No love. No deep feelings. No caring. Just the sisters and their sex toys. I knew the studs didn't respect us. In fact, I suspect they downright hate us. And I grew real tired of the whole trip."

"Is that why you wanted to leave the Leather Knights?" Rikki inquired.

Lex nodded, her red hair bobbing. "I just knew there must be a better place somewhere else. I planned to sneak out of the city, and my friend Mira agreed to come along. But you saw how far we got."

"How do the other residents of St. Louis feel about the Knights?" Rikki probed.

"They have to tolerate it because the Leather Knights protect them from outsiders," Lex detailed. "A lot of the people have what you might call normal families, but the sisters look down their noses at any woman who shares her life with a man. And the sisters never miss a chance to feed their lies to the little girls. Believe me, if a girl is told year after year that all men are scuzz, that men only want one thing from a woman and the only way to keep them in line is to make them into slaves, then the girl starts to accept all of this as true. I know. It happened to me."

"Do any of the other sisters feel the way you do?"

"Lots," Lex replied. "But they're too scared to defy Terza. They know what happens to traitors."

"Why is it," Rikki asked, "one sex is always trying to dominate the other? Why can't men and women learn to live in a state of mutual cooperation instead of antagonistic bickering?"

"How do the men and women get along at your Home?" Lex asked.

"We have our problems," Rikki said. "But from what I've seen, we relate much better than many men and women elsewhere. I don't think either side views the other as some sort of sex object. We're taught in the Family school to always seek for the inner beauty in every person. Having big breasts or a handsome face isn't a social advantage in the Family."

"I can't wait to see this Home of yours," Lex declared longingly.

"You will," Rikki promised. He stood and stretched his legs. "It's time to go."

"Where are we going?"

Rikki pointed down the hallway. "After Blade."

"Can't we give him more time?"

"No," Rikki said. "I've waited too long as it is. We'll search this building from top to bottom, every square inch. Do you have any idea where he could be?"

"You mean if they caught him?" Lex pondered a moment. "He might be in the holding cell, or maybe they're going to feed him to Grotto. Or Terza could be playing fun and games with him."

"We'll try the holding cell first," Rikki advised.

Lex took a deep breath and straightened. "I'm right behind you," she said, although she silently wished she were far away at Rikki's Home, where it was safe, where the men and women weren't constantly at each other's throats, where everyone tried to love one another.

Funny.

She'd assumed she was too mature to believe in fairy tales.

Lex shrugged her shoulders and stuck to Rikki's heels as he retraced their steps into the gloomy interior of the structure.

16

The gunfighter was in his element.

Hickok had been reared in the placid environment of the Home. He'd attended the Family school as required of all youngsters and teenagers, and been taught all of the profound spiritual truths the wise Elders knew. Although he perceived the validity of a doctrine such as "Love thy neighbor" intellectually, he found the practical applications left something to be desired. How was it possible, he often asked himself, to love your neighbor when that neighbor might be a scavenger intending to kill you and rob you, or a mutate bent on tearing you to shreds? He discreetly distinguished a flaw in such a philosophy. To him, it never made any sense for the spiritual people to allow themselves to be wiped out by their benighted brethren. There was only one viable alternative: the spiritual types, such as the Family, had to protect themselves from the manifold dangers proliferating after the unleashing of the nuclear and chemical holocaust. Early on, Hickok discovered his niche in life. He didn't think he was qualified to become a teacher or a preacher, but he knew he was more than competent to defend those who were spiritual from those who weren't.

Warrior status fit him like the proverbial glove.

Because he devoted his entire personality to whatever interested him, Hickok rapidly became one of the Family's top Warriors. His ambidextrous ability with handguns insured his prominence. And because he never fretted over the fate of the foes he downed in a gunfight, because he sincerely believed the Elders when they instructed him to accept the fact of survival beyond this initial life for anyone with the slightest shred of spiritual faith, he entertained few compunctions about pulling the trigger. In short, Hickok was one of the most proficient, and most deadly, Warriors in the Family. Some, such as Blade, insisted Hickok was *the* most deadly.

The Russians might have been inclined to agree.

Hickok spun and fired at the three soldiers coming through the glass doors. The AK-47 bucked and chattered, and the trio of troopers were struck before they could bring their own weapons to bear. They were catapulted backward by the impact of the heavy slugs tearing through their chests. The glass doors were hit too, and they shattered and crumbled with a loud crash.

There was no time to lose!

Four soldiers were still advancing from the direction of the hedgerow, and three were sprinting toward the gunman from the parking lot.

Hickok darted into the building, dodging the prone bodies blocking the doorway. He ran to the receptionist's desk and ducked behind it, straddling her unconscious form.

Footsteps pounded outside, and a moment later the seven soldiers raced into the receptionist's area.

Someone shouted orders in Russian.

Hickok tensed, wondering if they would look behind the desk or mistakenly suppose he had taken one of the corridors.

The footsteps tramped past the desk.

Hickok counted to three and rose, the AK-47 cradled at waist level.

The seven troopers were ten feet off and heading down one of the corridors.

"Peek-a-boo!" Hickok shouted.

To their credit, they tried to turn and shoot instead of diving for cover.

Hickok squeezed the trigger and swept the AK-47 in an arc. The soldiers were rocked and racked by the devastating hail of lead. Only one of them managed to return the gunman's fire, and he missed, his pistol plowing a shot into the desk in front of the Warrior.

Two of them screamed as they died.

All seven were sprawled on the tiled floor when the AK-47 went empty. Hickok tossed the gun aside and vaulted the desk. He ran to the glass doors and leaped over the three dead soldiers.

About a dozen people from the park, civilians by their attire, were tentatively congregating outside the Headquarters building.

Hickok charged them, drawing his Colts, hoping none of them was armed. They frantically parted as he jogged past, and then he was crossing a paved road and entering a large natural area with high, unkempt grass and a row of tall trees. He bypassed two children flying a kite and reached the safety of the trees.

No one was after him. Yet.

Hickok kept going, and once beyond the row of trees he paused to get his bearings.

That was when he saw it.

Whatever "it" was.

Off to his left, towering over the surrounding landscape, was a gigantic obelisk. The top portion was missing, apparently destroyed during the war, leaving a jagged crown at the crest.

What the blazes was it?

Hickok headed to the right. He spied a stand of trees 40 yards distant and made for them. He knew the soldiers would be after him in force, and he had to find a refuge quickly. But where? He didn't know the layout of the city. Were there any safe areas, sections

of the city inhabited only by descendants of the
original Americans? Or had the Russians imported
their own people to populate the city? And what
about the ones he saw in the park? Were they
Americans or Russians? For all he knew, he could be
alone in a city where every person was an enemy.

The gunman reached the trees.

Hickok dropped to his knees, holstering his
Pythons, gathering his breath. He saw a road yonder,
past the trees, and beyond the road a long lake or
pool.

Where the heck was he?

Frustrated, he slowly stood and walked to the edge
of the road. Directly ahead was the pool. To his right
was a wide, cleared space filled with pedestrians. To
his left, the road seemed to branch out and encircle
another pool. The air had a misty quality about it, and
he wondered if he was near a large body of water.

Which way should he go?

The Red Army would be sweeping the area any
minute. He decided to gamble, to mingle with the
masses, hoping he could lose himself in the crowd. He
walked from the trees and ambled parallel with the
long pool.

A young man and an attractive woman, seated on a
blue blanket with a wicker picnic basket by their side,
glanced up as he approached.

"Hi," the youth said.

"Howdy," Hickok greeted them.

The woman gawked at the gunman's waist and
nudged her companion. She whispered to him and his
brow knitted in consternation.

Hickok was five feet from them.

"Nice guns you have there," the youth commented
nervously.

"I like 'em," Hickok said.

"I thought guns were illegal," the youth stated.

"Not mine," Hickok assured him.

The youth and his lady friend exchanged hurried whispers.

Hickok passed them, his thumbs hooked in his gunbelt.

"Say, mister," the youth ventured.

Hickok stopped and looked over his left shoulder.

"We just heard some shooting," the youth said. "Was that you?"

Hickok scrutinized them, debating whether he could trust them.

"I've never seen anyone dressed like you before," the youth remarked, rubbing his hands on his jeans as he spoke. "You stand out like a sore thumb. It's none of my business, you understand, but if you're looking for somewhere you won't stick out, go around the west end of the Reflecting Pool, past the Lincoln Memorial, and go south. You'll come to Independence Avenue, and on the other side is West Potomac Park. They don't bother to cut the grass or trim the trees there and it's a real jungle."

"Why are you tellin' me this?" Hickok demanded.

"I can put two and two together," the youth said. "Gunshots. A stranger with a pair of revolvers." The youth lowered his voice. "I may not be with the Resistance, but that doesn't mean I like the Reds."

Hickok grinned. "Thanks, pard." He waved and walked toward the far end of the Reflecting Pool. What a stroke of luck! If he could reach West Potomac Park, he could lay over for a spell and figure out how to return to St. Louis. *That* was going to be the tough part. Evidently, they'd flown him from St. Louis to Washington, D.C., in just one night. The feat sounded impossible, but then he didn't know how fast one of those Red copters could fly. What was it General Malenkov had said? St. Louis was 860 miles from Washington? Did the Red Copters need to refuel en route? Seemed likely to him.

More people were in the vicinity of the Reflecting

Pool, enjoying the sunshine, idly strolling or chatting with friends. Several kids were floating wooden boats in the water.

Hickok realized he was attracting a lot of attention; nearly everyone was staring at him, a few going so far as to stop and gape. The residents he saw wore cheaply constructed clothing of an indeterminate fashion. None wore bucksins. And none packed hardware. That youth had been right on the money. He *did* stand out like a sore thumb.

The gunman reached the west end of the Reflecting Pool and paused, gazing at the edifice before him. The Lincoln Memorial, the youth had said. The structure was immense and impressive, with a massive dome and elaborate columns. Unlike the obelisk, the Lincoln Memorial hadn't been damaged during the war. A red banner with white lettering was suspended above the portal. The sign was in English:

"Lincoln, Champion of the Proletariat."

Hickok absently scratched his chin.

What the blazes was a proletariat?

"Excuse me, comrade," intruded an insistent voice.

Hickok swiveled to his right.

A stocky man in a blue uniform and carrying a nightstick was approaching.

"Howdy," Hickok said to him.

"What play are you with?" the man asked.

Play? Hickok casually placed his right hand on the right Python.

"I'm Dimitri, Capitol Police," the man said, smiling, revealing even spaced teeth. "I saw a play last year at the People's Center. You know, the old Kennedy Center. It was about the reign of Napoleon, and the costumes were fabulous. What play are you with?"

"*Scouts of the Prairie*," Hickok replied.

"When did it open?" the man asked, excited. "What is it about? I just love the plays!" he gushed. "There are so few anymore."

"It opens tonight," Hickok told him,. "At the . . . People's Center!"

"What is it about?" the policeman reiterated.

A flash of inspiration motivated the gunman. "It's all about how the Old West capitalists exploited the Indians and stole their land."

"Ahhhh, yes," the policeman stated. "We studied it in school. What part do you play? Your costume is most excellent."

"I play a man named Hickok," Hickok said. "He was what they called a gunfighter, or some such. It's a real exciting play."

"I can't wait to see it!" the policeman declared enthusiastically.

"Tell you what," Hickok said, leaning closer to the policeman. "I'm not supposed to do this, but I'll leave a message with the head honcho. Why don't you come and tell them Hickok sent you. I can promise you a time you won't forget. Bring the missus too."

"Free seats?" The policeman laughed, elated at his good fortune. "I can't thank you enough, comrade!"

Hickok shrugged, feigning humility. "That's what comrades are for, right?"

"Thank you just the same." The policeman continued on his rounds, whistling, content with the world.

Hickok turned from the Lincoln Memorial, bearing south. Yes, sir. There's no idiot like a happy idiot! He glanced behind him and detected a commotion at the eastern end of the Reflecting Pool.

Uh-oh.

Time to make tracks.

Hickok hurried, cutting across a lawn until he reached an avenue. Was it the one he wanted? Independence Avenue? There was no way of telling. But on the other side of the avenue was a veritable wall of vegetation, dense underbrush, and abundant trees.

The racket had reached the steps of the Lincoln Memorial.

Hickok looked both ways; nobody was nearby. Perfect! He ran across the avenue and into the bushes on the far side. The vegetation was thick, but negotiable. He pressed onward, keeping low, crawling under low limbs and protruding foliage or skirting them where possible. After 30 yards he stopped and listened.

Nothing behind him.

Maybe he had the breather he needed.

Hickok crept to the base of a spreading maple and leaned against the trunk.

So what was next?

The gunman thought of Blade and Rikki, and speculated on how they were faring in St. Louis. He certainly hoped they were doing better than he was. How would Sherry take it if he never returned to the Home? And what about little Ringo . . .

Hickok shook his head, annoyed at himself. Sure, he was in a tight scrape, but that was no reason to get all negative. He must look at the positive side of things.

There *had* to be a way out of this mess!

The air above abruptly became agitated by a stiff wind, and the tops of the trees started whipping from side to side as a funny "thupping" sound drew nearer and nearer.

Hickok drew his left Colt, craning his neck for a clear view through the tree limbs.

An enormous helicopter appeared, flying slowly to the southeast. It dwarfed the other helicopter Hickok had seen, the one responsible for flipping the SEAL on its side. This one was easily ten times as big. For a moment, the gunman believed the copter was searching for him, but it maintained a steady course to the southeast without deviating. A helicopter seeking him would be zigzagging all over the woods.

Where was it heading?

Hickok holstered his Python and rose. He hastened

after the copter, striving to keep it in sight, flinching as thorns bit into his legs and arms. He felt the helicopter might be landing close by. Why else would it be so low? He reached a small glade and stared upward.

The helicopter was descending toward the southeast.

He was right!

Hickok resumed running, ignoring the jabs and stabs from the sundry branches and twigs he passed. If he could reach that helicopter, and if he could force the pilot to fly him, he might be able to escape from Washington and head for St. Louis.

If.

If.

If.

Whoever invented that word should have been shot!

17

"The holding cell should be just ahead," Lex said.

Rikki nodded, a barely perceptible movement in the darkened hallway.

"I can't understand why we haven't seen any of the Knights," Lex whispered. "I doubt they gave up looking for us."

Rikki was bothered by the same consideration. Where *were* the Leather Knights? Even if Blade had been caught, it was doubtful the Knights would abandon their hunt for Lex and her "lover boy."

"I wish we were packing," Lex commented.

Rikki brandished the knife Blade had given him. "We're not defenseless," he reminded her.

"Oh, great," Lex said. "One lousy knife against all of their guns!"

A lantern hanging from a metal hook illuminated one of the recessed doors into the holding cell.

Rikki reached the door and gripped the doorknob. He listened, but all was quiet on the other side. Fully realizing he might be waltzing into a trap, he threw the door open. And there it was: the dirt floor, the balcony, the brick wall, and the chains.

But nothing else.

"We could try Terza's quarters," Lex recommended.

"Lead the way," Rikki said, stepping aside.

Lex crossed the holding cell to the far door. After ascertaining the hallway was unoccupied, she led

Rikki to the nearest stairs and up to the top floor of the library. "There might be guards," she whispered.

"I'll go first," Rikki offered. He cautiously opened the stairwell door and peered around the jamb.

A solitary Knight, a lean man with a crooked nose and armed with a holstered revolver, was leaning against the wall about ten feet from the stairwell. He appeared to be bored to death.

The knife in his right hand, Rikki eased from the stairwell and silently advanced toward the unsuspecting guard.

The Leather Knight raised his right hand and began examining his fingernails.

Rikki was eight feet from the guard.

The Knight coughed.

Six feet.

The Knight sensed another presence. Not anticipating trouble, he glanced to his right, his eyes widening in alarm at the sight of the small man in black.

"What the hell!" the Knight blurted out, and went for his gun.

Rikki was already in motion, leaping forward and sweeping his right hand back and out.

In the act of drawing his revolver, the Leather Knight was impaled in the throat. The horrifying shock of the knife in his neck stunned him. He opened his mouth to scream.

Rikki sprang, his legs arching upward in a graceful Yoko-tobi-geri, a side jump kick, his right foot, extended and rigid, slamming into the guard, catching his crooked nose dead center and smashing his head against the wall.

The guard grunted as his nostrils were crushed.

Rikki landed, his coiled frame in motion, spinning, executing a flawless Mawashi-geri, a roundhouse kick.

The guard was struck on his right cheek. He toppled

to the floor with a faint gasp.

Rikki looked at Lex. "Which room is it?" There were three doors on either side of the hallway.

Lex hastened to the closest door. She tried the knob. "It's not locked," she said, and shoved.

Rikki darted past her into the room.

It was empty.

"I don't get it," Lex stated. "I thought Terza was warm for Blade's form. Maybe she changed her mind about him. They might have decided to feed him to Grotto."

"Where?" Rikki asked.

"There's a special room downstairs hooked up to the sewers," Lex disclosed. "He might be there."

"Why the sewers?" Rikki inquired.

"That's where Grotto lives," Lex explained.

Rikki scanned the room. "We need weapons." He noticed a closet to the left of Terza's bed and walked to it.

"I'll keep watch," Lex offered, turning to the door, closing it.

Rikki opened the closet and found a dozen black-leather garments on wire hangers. Piled on the floor were sandals, black boots, and peculiar shoes with spiked heels. He closed the door and moved to rejoin Lex, but a pile of white clothing heaped on the floor by the bed attracted his attention.

"I hear voices!" Lex warned him.

Rikki knelt and touched the white clothing, a white-lace affair undoubtedly intended to expose more skin than it covered. About to stand, he detected a glimmer of silver from under the bed.

"They're coming this way!" Lex whispered urgently.

Rikki dropped to his knees and peeked under the bed. His pulse quickened at the discovery of the items he most wanted: Blade's Commando and Bowies and his own scabbard lying next to his katana. The Spirit was with them! He grabbed the scabbard and slid it through his black belt, then withdrew the katana from under the bed and with a practiced flourish returned the sword to its scabbard.

"They're almost here!" Lex said.

"Let them come," Rikki told her.

Lex turned from the doorway and glanced at him. "Why . . ." she began.

Rikki grinned and rose, the Commando and Bowies in his arms.

"Where did you . . ." Lex started to ask a question, then stopped as a loud shout filled the hallway.

Rikki ran to her side and handed over the Commando and the Bowies. "Hold these," he instructed her. He tiptoed to the door and pressed his left ear to the wood.

"—dead. Who the hell could have done it?" a man was demanding.

"The big guy is downstairs," mentioned another. "It has to be the runt or Lex."

"Let's check Terza's room," the first man said.

"I don't know," hedged the second. "She doesn't like anybody in her room without an invitation."

"She'll understand," declared the first man. "Come on."

Rikki motioned Lex away from the door. There were three lit lanterns in the room, and no time to extinguish them. He eased the katana from its scabbard and flattened behind the door.

Lex took cover behind the couch.

The door slowly opened, inch by inch. The barrel of a revolver materialized, jutting past the edge of the door.

"I don't see anyone," remarked the second man.

"We'd best check the whole room," said the first man.

Both studs entered, each with a revolver, and neither bothered to glance behind the open door.

"There ain't nobody here!" the second man groused.

Rikki rushed from concealment, his katana streaking up and in.

The first stud, a short man with a flowing mustache, never knew what hit him. The katana angled into his neck, severing half of his throat, causing large quantities of blood to gush from the cut vessels and pour over his chest and legs.

Rikki didn't wait for the first man to collapse. He took two lightning steps and aimed a slash at the second man.

The second stud crouched and whirled, pointing his revolver at the man in black. He was squeezing the trigger when the sword hacked his gunhand from his wrist.

Anyone could have heard his shriek a mile away.

Rikki finished him with a well-placed reverse thrust into the stud's heart.

The Knight gurgled, spitting up blood and bile, and tumbled to the carpet.

Lex emerged from hiding. She had seen the entire encounter by looking around the lower corner of the couch.

"We must hurry to Blade," Rikki said.

Lex nodded. "I hope you show me how to do that someday."

Rikki wiped his katana on the second stud's black vest. "Considerable practice is required."

"It'd be worth it," Lex said. "If I get half as good as you, no one would dare mess with me again."

"Take me to Grotto," Rikki directed her.

"What am I going to do about these knives?" Lex asked, referring to the Bowies. "I'm liable to poke myself before we get there."

Rikki debated a moment. Both Bowies and the Commando were quite an armful. When the Knights had stripped Blade's weapons, they'd merely removed the Bowies from their sheaths. So Lex was compelled to carry the Bowies with their keen blades exposed.

"I'll take them," Rikki volunteered. He carefully aligned each knife under his belt, insuring the belt supported each knife by its guard, and slanted their points away from his privates.

"That doesn't look too safe," Lex remarked, worried by the proximity of the knives to his groin.

"Just hope I don't sneeze," Rikki joked. "Come on."

They left Terza's room on the double, Rikki leading until they had descended the stairs to the bottom floor. Lex took over, cradling the Commando in her arms, making for the pit room where Grotto was fed. The hallways were a virtual maze, and Rikki chafed at the delay.

"Isn't there a shortcut?" he asked at one point.

Lex stopped. "I'm sticking to the halls we don't use too often. We might avoid the Knights this way."

Rikki glanced at the Commando. "Have you checked it to see if it's loaded?"

"Damn! Never thought of it!" Lex admitted. She fiddled with the magazine release until the magazine popped free. She held it in her left hand and studied it by the light of a nearby lantern. "The clip is full," she announced, "but I don't have a spare."

"Blade usually carries those in his pockets," Rikki informed her.

Lex replaced the magazine in the Commando.

"Will we be there soon?" Rikki asked.

"Pretty soon," Lex replied.

The sound of many voices in turmoil abruptly came from behind them.

"What's that?" Lex whispered.

The turmoil was growing louder.

Lex motioned for Rikki to follow. They raced along the passage until they reached a branch, and she took a right.

The voices weren't far off.

Rikki drew Lex into the darkest shadows.

"—tell you I saw them!" a woman was bellowing angrily.

"Sure you did," another woman responded.

"But I did!" insisted the first. "About two hundred yards back. I saw them pass a junction."

"Then where the hell are they?" demanded yet a third woman.

"If we haven't seen them by now," chimed in a stud, "we'll never catch them."

"If they were ever there," griped one of the women.

"I saw them, damn you!" insisted the first woman.

There were eight of them, five sisters and three studs, and they reached the fork in the tunnels and stopped. None of them ventured into the branch concealing Rikki and Lex.

"So where do we go from here?" inquired one of the sisters.

"I'm tired of looking," said another. "Why don't we grab a bite to eat? I'm starving!"

"Will you listen to yourselves?" snapped the fifth woman. "They would hear us coming a mile off."

"So what do we do?" asked a stud.

"Let's try this way," suggested a sister, and entered the right branch.

A whirlwind in black, wielding a scintillating blade, pounced on them from the shadows. In the three seconds they required to react to the onslaught, four of them were dead. A stud whipped his pistol from its holster, but that streaking sword was lanced through his right eye and into his brain before he could fire. The sister responsible for initially glimpsing Rikki and Lex successfully pulled her revolver, but the katana bit into her forehead, slicing off the top of her head, hair and all, and she uttered an uncanny death cry as she fell.

Hidden in the shadows, Lex watched in dazed fascination, dazzled by Rikki's prowess with the katana. His sinewy body was a twisting, flowing dervish of destruction. To her untrained eye, it seemed as if he executed his movements without conscious deliberation, as if he and the sword were one.

Thirty seconds after they entered the right branch, the eight Leather Knights were dead.

Rikki cleaned his katana on a stud's pants and rejoined Lex.

Lex stared at him with unconcealed admiration. "I'm beginning to wonder if anyone can kill you," she said by way of a compliment.

"Anyone can kill me," Rikki stated. "We all die, sooner or later. It's the technique for translating our souls from this world to the next."

Lex wanted to reach out and touch him, to smother his lips with fiery kisses. Instead, she chuckled. "You're all right, you know that?"

"I do now," Rikki replied, smiling. Then he turned serious. "We must reach Blade as quickly as possible."

Lex nodded. "Come on."

They jogged along the tunnels, sometimes taking a right fork, sometimes a left.

"How far underground are we?" Rikki asked once.

"I don't know," Lex responded. "But Grotto's room is the last one we built."

"It would be," Rikki remarked.

After a series of winding hallways, Lex slowed and pointed to a wall ahead. "That's it."

"A dead end?" Rikki queried, perplexed.

"Not really," Lex said. "The door is hidden in the wall. It's one of our secret retreats in case the Reds ever invade St. Louis."

Rikki ran to the brick wall.

Lex checked to verify no one was in pursuit, then joined him.

"How do we get in?" Rikki whispered.

Lex groped over the wall, seeking the false brick, the one covering the latch for the door. "It should be here somewhere."

"I pray nothing has happened to Blade," Rikki said anxiously.

"I bet he's okay," Lex said optimistically.

A tremendous roar shook the wall, emanating from the other side.

"I can't find the latch!" Lex wailed.

18

Hickok crouched in the high grass bordering the former East Potomac Park and surveyed the airstrip. He knew this area had once been the East Potomac Park because he'd stumbled across a faded, weather-beaten sign at the side of Buckeye Drive, a sign replete with a miniature map of the Tidal Basin and the tract east of the Potomac River.

He'd been lucky so far.

Real lucky.

Hickok had been able to keep the helicopter in sight as it flew from the West Potomac Park, over the Jefferson Memorial, and landed at the airstrip. Traveling undetected from the West Potomac Park to the airstrip had been painstaking and arduous. Fortunately, the Jefferson Memorial had been leveled during World War III; all that remained were several shattered columns and the cracked and ruined dome lying on the ground. Hickok was glad the structure had been razed. Otherwise, he might have encountered large crowds similar to those near the Lincoln Memorial. He silently thanked the Spirit as he crept toward the airstrip, using every available cover.

Once, as he was nearing Buckeye Drive, a squad of soldiers had tramped past his position. They were marching toward the Washington Channel.

Hickok had crossed Buckeye and hidden in the grass, and now he was only 15 feet from the northwestern perimeter of the strip. He parted the grass in front of him for a better look-see.

The airstrip was loaded with helicopters. Huge helicopters. Small helicopters like the one the SEAL had engaged. And medium-sized helicopters. Some had single rotors. Others, especially the immense ones, had twin rotors, one above each end of the whirlybird. Technicians and flight personnel crowded the airstrip. Several tanker trucks, evidently conveying fuel, arrived on departed at periodic intervals.

After he had observed the proceedings for a spell, Hickok's interest was aroused by one particular copter. It was one of the largest on the airstrip, and the hub of intense activity. Hickok deduced they were preparing the helicopter for takeoff. A red tanker truck had pulled up, and three men were involved in running a hose from the tanker to the copter. Other men were engrossed in loading supplies onto the helicopter. One of the items Hickok saw rang a mental bell.

What was it General Malenkov had said?

"Our helicopter will use a winch and a sling and fly it here."

Hickok was familiar with winches. The Family Tillers used small winches to store bales of hay and other perishables in F Block. So when he saw a gigantic winch mounted above the bay doors on the huge helicopter being serviced by the tanker truck, a surge of excitement pulsed through him.

What if it were the one they were planning to use to transport the SEAL to Washington?

Several minutes later, his hunch was confirmed. Two events took place. First, a steel, sling-like affair was placed aboard the copter. And secondly, Leiutenant Voroshilov drove up in a jeep.

Now what would General Malenkov's pet flunky be doing here?

Lieutenant Voroshilov carefully inspected the

tandem helicopter, apparently guaranteeing the ship was airworthy. To Hickok, it seemed as if the lieutenant spent an inordinate amount of time involved in the task. Voroshilov even climbed a ladder to examine the rotors. Wouldn't that task normally be a job for one of the noncommissioned types? the gunman asked himself. If so, why did Lieutenant Voroshilov devote so much energy to the work?

A troop transport approached the helicopter from the direction of a building situated along the Washington Channel. The brakes squealed as the truck stopped. Six soldiers emerged from the rear of the transport and formed a line.

Lieutenant Voroshilov walked up to the soldiers and returned the salute of a big man at the end of the line. They conversed for a moment, then the lieutenant walked back to the copter and the six men stood at ease.

Hickok thoughtfully gnawed on his lower lip. Those six must be the men Voroshilov was taking on the mission. He speculated on whether the copter would be departing soon, or if they would wait for nightfall. Considering the bustle of activity, they probably intended to take off soon.

Not so good.

If they waited for dark, he might easily slip aboard and hitch a ride to the SEAL. In a helicopter that tremendous, with so many crates and boxes being stacked in the cargo bay, it would be a cinch to hide out until they reached their destination.

But what if they didn't wait for night?

Hickok surveyed his surroundings. About 15 feet away was the edge of the airstrip. About 20 feet beyond rested an unattended small helicopter. About 40 feet past the small whirlybird was the tanker truck. And then came the jumbo copter.

How the blazes was he going to get from—

A portly military man was walking toward the small helicopter, a clipboard in his left hand. He whistled as he walked, and as he neared the copter he consulted his clipboard.

Hickok lowered his body until just his eyes were elevated. What was this hombre up to with the small copter?

The man peered inside the helicopter's bubble, studying the instrument panel. Then he slowly walked around the aircraft.

Hickok glanced in both directions.

None of the technicians or other personnel was nearby.

The gunman waited until the military man had his back to him, and then he charged, sprinting forward, his moccasins nearly soundless on the hard tarmac.

At the last second, the man with the clipboard sensed someone was behind him and started to turn.

Hickok rammed his right hand against the man's head, driving the soldier's skull into the helicopter bubble.

There was a resounding crack, and the clipboard clattered to the blacktop. The man weaved back and forth, then slumped to the ground, a trail of crimson descending from the right side of his head.

Hickok knelt and scanned the airstrip.

No one had noticed.

Yet.

Hickok's vanquished antagonist was less than an inch shorter than the gunman, but his limbs were heftier and his stomach was downright paunchy.

Might do.

Hickok hastily removed the soldier's clothing, then his own gunbelt, and hurriedly donned the uniform, covering his buckskins. The shoulders and elbows felt a bit tight, but they adequately hid his buckskins and that was the important thing. Although the pants were too short, with the hem two inches above his ankles, Hickok decided to risk it anyway and hope the ill-fitting uniform was inconspicuous.

But what to do about the Pythons and the gunbelt?

Hickok frowned. There was no way he could wear the gunbelt in the open; the Reds would spot him right off. He could tuck the Colts under his belt, under the uniform shirt. And he could stuff the bullets from the gunbelt in his pockets. But where did that leave the gunbelt?

There was a sharp retort from the huge tandem helicopter, a mechanical coughing and sputtering, and suddenly the two rotors began to rotate.

They were getting set to leave!

Blast! Hickok reluctantly extracted his spare ammo from the gunbelt and filled his pants pockets. He dropped the gunbelt on the ground next to the unconscious soldier.

"Think of it as a trade for the duds," the gunman said.

The rotors were increasing their revolutions, and a distinct hum carried on the breeze.

Hickok scooped up the clipboard and jogged around the small copter.

It was now or never!

The hose had been secured on the red tanker, and the three men were standing near the truck watching the tandem helicopter.

Hickok raced for the copter.

Lieutenant Voroshilov was nowhere in sight. The six troopers had likewise disappeared.

The rotors were revolving at a fantastic clip.

Hickok passed the red tanker and darted toward the helicopter. The cargo bay doors were still open, and he angled for them, waving the clipboard over his head.

One of the troopers stepped into view, framed in the cargo doors. He was reaching for one of the doors, intending to close them, when he spotted the blond man with the clipboard.

Hickok plainly saw the confused expression on the soldier's face. He smiled up at the trooper as he neared the cargo doors.

The tandem helicopter started to rise.

No!

Hickok estimated there were ten feet to go. He took three bounding steps and leaped, his arms extended, his fingers outstretched, discarding the clipboard as he clutched at the helicopter. He gripped the lower edge of the cargo bay and held on for dear life.

The helicopter was ascending at a rapid speed.

Hickok could feel his body swaying in the wind as his hands threatened to be torn from his wrists.

The tandem copter was 20 feet up and climbing.

Hickok grimaced as he attempted to clamber aboard. He wanted to hook his elbows, then swing his legs up, but the helicopter abruptly changed direction, swinging from a southeasternly heading to a westerly course. The motion caused the gunman to slip and sag, and his left hand lost most of its hold. He made a valiant effort to haul himself up, but his tenuous grasp was unequal to the endeavor.

He was going to fall!

The copter was 60 feet up and still rising.

Hickok's left arm slipped free, and for a few precarious seconds he dangled from his right arm, envisioning what it would be like to be splattered all over the landscape below.

Sturdy hands clasped the gunfighter's right wrist, and he was unceremoniously lifted into the cargo bay, scraping his shins as he was hauled onto his back.

Two soldiers straddled him. One of them, the one he'd seen in the doorway earlier, was holding an AK-47 pointed at the gunman's chest.

Hickok almost went for his Pythons. But they were under the uniform shirt and their barrels were wedged under his belt. He knew the trooper would blast him before he could whip the Colts clear.

The one with the Ak-47 said some words to the Warrior in what Hickok assumed was Russian.

Hickok grinned.

The trooper repeated his sentence.

Hickok grinned wider.

The soldier leaned over and pressed the barrel of the AK-47 against the gunman's nose. "I will use English," the trooper stated. "I think I know who you are, and if you so much as twitch one of your little muscles, I will blow your nose off!"

19

Blade was beginning to think Grotto would never appear.

Hours had passed. Six more Leather Knights had joined the others already in the room. They took turns pounding the board against the side of the pit. Twice Blade had tried to initiate a conversation, but each time Terza had ordered him to shut his mouth. She became testier as the hours lengthened, pacing the lip of the pit, her hands entwined in the small of her back.

"Maybe Grotto ain't gonna show," Cardew said, voicing the thought most of the assembled Knights entertained.

"He'll show!" Terza barked.

"He's taken a long time before," Erika interjected. "Probably because he was far off in the sewers. But the damn thing has never taken this long."

"He'll show!" Terza repeated.

"What's the big deal?" Erika demanded. "So what if we don't feed this bastard to Grotto today? There's always tomorrow."

Terza ceased her nervous pacing and glared at Erika. "We're not leaving this room until Grotto shows."

"But why?" Erika insisted. "We're getting hungry. Why don't we call it quits for today?"

Terza's hands drifted to her Comanches. "Are you questioning my judgment?"

Erika retreated a step. "Now you hold on—"

"Are you telling me what to do?" Terza asked in a menacing tone.

Erika paled. "No. No! Of course I ain't! I didn't mean nothin' by it! Honest!"

Terza scanned the room. "Anybody else got anything they'd like to say?"

None of the Knights responded.

"Keep poundin'!" Terza shouted at the stud with the board, who had stopped while Erika and Terza were arguing.

"One big, happy hamily," Blade said.

Terza turned and faced him. "Another word out of you, asshole, and I won't wait for Grotto! I'll do the job myself!"

"Big talk when you're armed and I'm not," Blade boldly replied.

Terza took a step toward the Warrior, the right Comanche easing upward.

A sibilant hissing filled the room, the same hissing sound they had heard earlier in the day.

"I hope the damn thing shows up this time," Erika muttered.

The damn thing did.

Blade had seen many mutants over the years. Deformed and demented, they came in all shapes and sizes. Often they beggared description. There were the mutates themselves—former reptiles, amphibians, and mammals, transformed into ravenous, pus-covered horrors. There were the insects and their close kin, subject to rare strains of deviate giantism, thought to be a genetic imbalance caused by one of the chemical-warfare weapons employed during the Big Blast, or a combination of the chemicals and the massive radiation. There were numerous other . . . things . . . as well.

This was one of them.

A red snout appeared, visible in the subterranean

entrance to the pit.

"Grotto!" Erika said, sounding relieved.

Blade tensed, enthralled and repulsed simultaneously.

The red snout was at least four feet wide and two feet high. Slowly, the creature creeped into the pit. Its eyes and head seemed to fill the entrance, its eyes a luminous brown, wide and unblinking, while its head was a grotesque, bloated caricature of a beast vaguely reptilian or amphibious by nature. More of the mutant emerged. Its skin was a bright red, crisscrossed with black stripes. The stocky legs were short in relation to the rest of the body, and its clawed feet were webbed. The body was bulky, bulging with raw power. Its thick tail was equally as long as the head and body combined. Tiny holes just behind the eyes served as ears, and its mouth was a thin slit from ear to ear. The monstrosity entered the pit and stopped, hissing, while a putrid stench hovered in the air.

Blade estimated the creature was close to ten feet in height and about seven feet wide. The mouth was large enough to swallow him in two bites.

Terza, Erika, Cardew, and some of the other Leather Knights were poised at the edge of the pit, admiring their "pet." Every Knight in the room was gaping at it.

Blade was completely, momentarily, forgotten.

Blade saw his opening, and he took it. Warrior training encompassed years of intense instruction in the many facets of combat and war. One aspect was deliberately stressed by the Elders responsible for teaching the Warriors the tricks of their trade. As one Elder put it: "In a fight, in any life-or-death situation, victory is frequently predicted on recognizing the enemy's weaknesses, on using your foes mistakes against them. All they have to do is lower their guard for a split-second, and their defeat is assured if you take advantage of their mistake. Always remember: if someone is trying to kill you or any other Family member, your primary responsibility is to your Family and yourself. Do whatever is necessary to win. You won't get a second chance."

So coordinated was Blade, so instantaneous his reflexes, that he was in motion even as he perceived his advantage. He took four steps and reached Terza and Erika. The two Knights, concentrating on the hideous Grotto, were unaware of his presence until a steely hand pounded each of them on the back and they were propelled over the edge of the pit, Erika screaming in terror.

Blade whirled, his granite fist crashing into Cardew's right cheek.

The stud tottered backward and collapsed.

Petrified shrieks were coming from the pit as Blade spun and attacked a nearby sister.

The other Leather Knights began to react. Initially stunned by the sight of Terza and Erika falling into the pit, they recovered and attacked the giant Warrior. One of the studs went to use his rifle, but rejected the idea when he saw how close his target was to several of his friends.

Blade slugged the sister in the abdomen, and kneed her in the face when she doubled over.

Spouting blood from her pulverized nose, the sister catapulted backward.

Blade was tackled by a stud. He felt arms encircle his legs, and he was borne to the ground by the impact. He desperately threw his body to the left to avoid being knocked into the pit, and he succeeded in digging his elbows and forearms into the very edge before arresting his momentum. Hovering on the brink of the hole, he glanced down.

A pair of slim legs protruded from the corners of Grotto's gaping maw, and rivulets of blood poured over its lower jaw.

Terza?

Blade couldn't waste time speculating on the identity of the deceased. The stud holding his legs was striving to push him over the edge. Blade glanced over his right shoulder, noting his opponent's head was just below his buttocks, and he twisted, rolling to the left, throwing his entire weight into the movement.

The stud's grip slipped, and he lunged for the Warrior's waist.

Blade reached back and down with his right hand, his calloused fingers grasping the stud's long black hair and yanking the Knight's head upward.

The stud cried out as his neck was wrenched. He felt as if his neck were being torn from his shoulders. Cursing, he pummeled the iron arm clutching his hair, to no avail.

Blade heaved, drawing the stud higher until they were eye to eye.

The Knight attempted to punch Blade in the face.

Blade sneered as he rose to his knees. He placed his left hand under the stud's chin, braced his coiled arms, and savagely snapped his hands to the right.

Several of the stud's vertebrae fractured with an audible crack.

Two other Knights, both sisters, pounced on the Warrior, one from the left, the other from the right, clasping his wrists and trying to force him into the pit.

Blade flexed his arms and strained, throwing his arms forward and tossing the sisters over the lip of the pit. They screeched as they fell.

Pandemonium was rampant in the room. Some of the Leather Knights were converging on their prisoner. Others were bolting for the door. A few were perched on the rim of the pit, guns at the ready, watching Grotto. As Blade rose to his feet, the pandemonium was compounded by three developments. Grotto clawed at the pit, scrambling to climb to the top. The mutant raised its bloated head and voiced a thunderous roar, shaking the walls and causing dirt to crumble from the sides of the pit. Three of the sisters reached the door and frantically threw it open. Almost immediately, a diminutive figure in black scooted into the room, a flashing sword in his hands, and with three glimmering strokes he dispatched the trio.

It was Rikki!

Blade started toward his fellow Warrior, but a stud came at him, a knife in the Knight's right hand.

Grotto was in a frenzy, hissing and roaring as it attempted to reach the pit rim. Its rear legs dug into the side, spraying dirt in every direction. It gave a stupendous heave and its front legs obtained a purchase on the pit edge, not more than eight feet from the Warrior.

Blade, concentrating on his adversary with the knife, failed to see Grotto's achievement. He dodged a wild swing of the knife and retreated a step, moving three feet nearer to the creature's salivating jaws.

Near the door, a stud with a rifle sighted on the swordsman in black, but a redheaded woman burst into the room, her machine gun chattering, and the stud's chest was stitched by a line of heavy slugs.

Lex had entered the fray.

Blade backed up another step as the stud with the knife lunged again.

Grotto's head and shoulders were clear of the pit and his body was still rising.

Rikki spotted Blade's danger, but before he could race to his friend's aid he was confronted by two sisters, both with drawn revolvers.

One of the sisters fired.

Rikki grimaced as his right side was creased, the bullet tearing a furrow in his ribs. He doubled over, feigning acute anguish, and when the sisters closed in to finish him off, he suddenly straightened, slashing the katana from right to left, hacking off the first woman's left arm, her gun arm, and cleaving open the second woman's stomach. The first woman seemed petrified by the loss of her arm: her terrified eyes frozen on the sight of her blood pumping from the severed stump. She barely noticed when another slash of the katana split her forehead, and she was dead before her body struck the ground. The second woman dropped her revolver and spread her hands over her ruptured stomach, futilely endeavoring to prevent her intestines and other organs from spilling out. The sword strike through her heart was anticlimatic.

Blade ducked yet another knife swipe, and caught the stud's wrist in his powerful hands. He swept his right knee up into the stud's elbow, and heard the pop as it cracked.

The stud grunted and tried to jerk free.

Blade floored him with a right cross. He saw Rikki heading his way and took a step toward him, but a strident roar stopped him in his tracks. He whirled.

Grotto was almost on top of the pit. Except for its pumping rear legs and tail, it was actually out of the pit, squatting on the rim.

Damn!

Blade broke into a run, making for Rikki.

Lex downed two of the Knights with a burst from the Commando. The sole Knight left in the room, a tall blonde sister, was cowering against one wall.

Rikki darted toward Blade, but he was still 12 feet away when Grotto surged over the rim of the pit and went after the giant Warrior.

Rikki grabbed the hilt of one of the Bowies. "Catch!" he shouted, and tossed the knife.

Blade deftly caught the Bowie on the fly with his right hand.

Rikki threw the other Bowie.

Blade stopped, his keen eyes following the knife's trajectory, and his left hand plucked it from the air with deceptive ease. He spun, sensing the monster was right behind him.

He was right.

Grotto was six feet from the Warrior, its mouth wide open, displaying upper and lower rows of small but pointed teeth. The motion of its ungainly legs and tail caused the creature to weave from side to side as it advanced. The first bite of its gruesome jaws closed on empty space.

Blade leaped to the right as the creature attacked, driving his left Bowie up and in, under the mutant's jawbone, into the fleshy area fringing the thick neck.

Grotto recoiled, feeling the pain, jerking his head away from the Bowie.

Knowing he would be too exposed if he tried to flee, Blade opted for the unexpected. He aggressively charged forward, under Grotto's neck, and buried both of his Bowies in the thing's vulnerable underbelly.

Grotto roared and scrambled to the right, not far from the pit, hissing as it swiveled and snapped at the puny human.

Blade felt the creature's foul breath on his face, like the rank stink of a decayed corpse, and flung himself backwards.

Grotto's teeth crunched together mere inches from its prey.

Blade stumbled, landing on his left knee. He saw Grotto rushing him, and he extended the Bowies to meet the assault.

A streak of masterfully crafted steel sliced the mutant from its neck to its shoulder as Rikki came to Blade's rescue. Green fluid sprayed from the wound, spattering the Warrior in black.

Grotto turned to face this new threat, enraged. Its jaw distended, it pounced.

Rikki rolled, avoiding the cavernous maw, and came up with the katana in a swirling motion, tearing open the side of Grotto's face. He backpedaled, scurrying to Blade's side.

"Glad you could make it," Blade quipped.

"Wouldn't have missed this for the world," Rikki rejoined.

Further conversation was precluded by Grotto; the mutant bellowed and charged the two Warriors.

Blade dived to the right, toward the pit, while Rikki sprinted to the left.

Grotto hesitated for a moment, uncertain of which victim to pursue. It snarled and went after Rikki.

The Family's consummate martial artist held his ground.

Grotto reached its quarry and hissed, spreading its jaws, its tongue flicking outward in spasmodic anticipation.

Rikki swung, slashing his katana up and around, the keen blade severing a third of the creature's tongue from its mouth.

Grotto recoiled and uttered a rumbling, shrill cry. It lashed its head from side to side, in misery, tormented by the loss of its tongue.

Blade found himself standing behind the monster, not four feet from its tail. He saw Rikki take another swipe with his sword, and Grotto try to take Rikki's head off. Rikki avoided the slavering jaws, but his left foot caught on the leg of a slain Leather Knight prone on the ground, and he lost his balance. He fell, landing on his left side.

Grotto roared and surged forward.

A desperate plan, a blaze of inspiration, pervaded Blade's consciousness, and with the idea came action. He ran toward Grotto, and when just three feet from the creature's tail he leaped, his coiled leg muscles carrying him over Grotto's tail onto its back, at the junction of the tail and the spinal column. His knees clamped on the tail, as he sank his Bowies to the hilt in the genetic deviate's back.

Grotto stiffened, then whipped its tail in an arc, striving to dislodge the man-thing.

Blade was clipped by the broad tail. He felt something hard strike his left shoulder, and he was knocked forward, the Bowies wrenching clear of the mutant's rancid flesh. He rolled twice and came up on his knees, perched on Grotto's squat neck.

Grotto snapped its head up and down, shaking its whole body, attepting to toss the man off.

Rikki closed in and delivered a deep slash to Grotto's throat.

Blade, clinging to the pliant skin on Grotto's neck with all of his strength, racked his brain for a means of destroying the creature. There had to be a way! But how? It had sustained several severe injuries, it was pumping a sickly green fluid from its body by the gallon, and yet still it fought on, endowed with a fearless nature and a ravenous appetite. The Bowies and the katana seemed unable to deliver a death blow. Where would it be most vulnerable? In the heart? Where would the heart be located in a creature of this size? All these thoughts passed through his mind in the twinkling of an instant.

And then it hit him.

There was a way!

Blade lunged forward, wrapping his legs around the mutant's neck. He extended the Bowies as far as his arms could reach, one on each side of the creature's face, one next to each eye.

"Do it!" he heard Lex scream.

Blade plunged the Bowies into Grotto's brown orbs, all the way in, and twisted.

Grotto reacted as if electrified by a bolt of lightning, its huge form convulsing and contorting, hissing all the while, its head shaking from right to left and up and down.

Blade could scarcely retain his grip. He felt the creature moving from side to side, and he could see Rikki yelling something to him, but he couldn't hear the words over Grotto's hissing.

Grotto's violent throes intensified.

"—pit! The pit!" Rikki yelled in alarm.

The pit?

The pit!

Blade jerked the Bowies free and rolled to the right, off of Grotto's neck. Something collided with his back, and he was sent flying, arms and legs flailing in the air, to crash onto the ground in a daze. He shook his head to clear his fuzzy mind, and rose to his hands and knees.

"Are you all right?" asked a concerned male voice.

Blade looked up.

Rikki smiled at him. "The Family will tell this tale for generations."

Blade glanced around, confused, disoriented. "Where . . ."

"The pit," Rikki answered before Blade could complete his question.

Blade stumbled to his feet. He tottered to the edge of the pit, his whole body aching like hell, and peered over the edge.

Grotto was lying in the center of the pit, on its side, its mouth open and slack, its eyes pools of green fluid, its legs curled up, its tail quivering.

Grotto was dead.

"I never saw anything like that!" Lex said as she joined them. "I wanted to shoot," she added, holding up the Commando, "but I was afraid I'd hit one of you."

Blade nodded absently, not yet fully recovered, staring at the creature on the pit floor.

"Are you all right?" Rikki repeated.

"Just a little dazed," Blade responded.

"Its head hit you as you were rolling off," Rikki disclosed.

Blade glanced at the black hole in the side of the pit, the hole providing access to the sewers. "Terza told me there are more of those things down there," he commented in a low voice.

"Yeah," Lex confirmed. "So?"

"So sooner or later those things are going to start coming out of the sewers to feed," Blade predicted.

"A few have already done it," Lex stated. "What's the big deal?"

Blade stared at her, sweat beading his brow. "Population growth is going to force more and more of them to take to the streets," he said wearily. "From what we've seen in our travels, many cities are like St. Louis. Living in them may become untenable."

Lex gazed at Grotto, frowning. "So what? I don't like living here anyway."

Rikki touched Blade on the left elbow. "We should be leaving."

Blade nodded. He realized he was still holding the Bowies, and he held them up. They were covered with the sticky green fluid. "Yuck," he said, and walked to a fallen sister.

Rikki scanned the room. "We are the only ones here," he observed.

Blade wiped his knives clean on the sister's black-leather vest. "You can bet reinforcements are on the way."

"You can have this," Lex offered, extending the Commando. "I'll take one of the rifles."

Blade sheathed his Bowies and took the Commando. "Thanks." He paused. "I appreciate all of the assistance you've rendered. And I know how you feel about living in St. Louis. How would you like to come and live with us?"

Lex grinned. "Rikki already made me the same offer."

"And?"

"And the sooner we get to this Home of yours," Lex said, "the better."

Blade smiled. "Lead the way."

Lex took a rifle from a dead stud, and found a handful of ammunition in his right front pocket. "Rikki told me you guys are called Warriors," she mentioned as she straightened.

"There are fifteen Warriors," Blade affirmed.

Lex swept the room with her right hand. "And you Warriors do this kind of thing all the time?"

"It does seem to happen a lot," Blade admitted. "Why?"

"Oh, nothing," Lex said. "But after seeing what you guys do for a living, I can't help but wonder what you do for kicks."

20

This was another blasted mess he'd gotten himself into!

The gunman was seated on a long bench on one side of the cargo bay. Across from him, on another wooden bench, sat five Red soldiers, each with an AK-47, each pointing their weapon in his general direction. Nearby, toward the rear of the aircraft, boxes and crates and miscellaneous equipment were stacked to the ceiling. In the opposite direction, a narrow alley between more crates and boxes led to a closed door. The sixth Red, the one he'd first seen in the cargo bay doorway and evidently a sergeant or of some equivalent rank, had disappeared through the door mere minutes before. After the sergeant and one other trooper had hoisted the gunfighter into the helicopter, they'd shoved him to the bench and ordered him to sit.

But the rascals had made a serious mistake.

Hickok wanted to laugh. The cowchips had neglected to search him for weapons. Consequently, the Pythons were safely tucked under his belt, hidden by the bulky uniform shirt over his buckskins.

"Any of you gents feel like shootin' the breeze?" Hickok amiably inquired.

None of them responded.

"I have a pard by the name of Joshua," Hickok genially told them. "He once told me a motto of his. You bozos could learn from it. If you ever want to make friends, old Josh once said, you've got to be friendly. You jokers sure ain't the friendly type."

One of the Reds wagged his AK-47. "Shut your mouth. We are not your friends."

"Why do we have to be enemies?" Hickok countered. "The war was a hundred years ago."

"The war is not over until Communism has conquered the globe," the soldier said.

Hickok sighed. "You must be minus a few marbles. There ain't no way you turkeys will conquer the world."

"In time we will," the trooper said confidently.

"You're breakin' wind."

The soldier's eyebrows narrowed. "Breakin' wind?"

"Do you really expect the folks to just roll over and play dead while you run roughshod over 'em?" Hickok asked. "If you do, you must be eatin' locoweed on a regular basis."

The trooper was about to speak, but the door toward the front of the aircraft opened. The sergeant returned, followed by a familiar figure. They approached the gunman.

"Hello, Hickok," Lieutenant Voroshilov greeted the warrior. "This is a surprise."

"Not as big of a surprise as I wanted," Hickok said.

"I just finished talking to General Malenkov on the radio," Lieutenant Voroshilov revealed. "He was equally surprised. It seems we underestimated you."

"So how soon before we get back to Washington?" Hickok asked.

"We are not turning around," Lieutenant Voroshilov disclosed.

Hickok's own surprise registered on his features. "Why not? I reckon the general is a mite eager to get his paws on me."

Lieutenant Voroshilov nodded. "He is most desirous of talking with you again," he said. "Only the next time it will be different. Your escape angered the general. He is going to have his . . . consultants . . . question you next time. Perhaps you have heard of them? They are the KGB."

Hickok shrugged. "Never heard of 'em."

"Why don't you relax," Lieutenant Voroshilov suggested. "We will be in the air several hours before we refuel."

"Why aren't you takin' me back to Washington?" Hickok inquired.

Lieutenant Voroshilov sat down on the bench alongside the gunman. His green eyes studied the warrior, as if he were examining an inferior life-form. "Several reasons. Precious fuel would be wasted by the return flight, and fuel is one resource we cannot afford to waste."

"Don't have a lot of it, huh?" Hickok interrupted.

"Not as much as we would like," Voroshilov said. "We have two refineries in operation, but they can't supply enough fuel for all our needs."

"Why don't you just get some more from Russia?" Hickok queried.

Voroshilov's mouth tightened. "If only we could."

"Why can't you?" Hickok pressed him.

Voroshilov considered the question for a while. "I see no reason why I can't tell you. The information isn't classified, and you won't live to pass it on." He thoughtfully stared at the closed cargo bay doors. "We lost touch with our motherland thirty years ago."

"What? You're kiddin'," Hickok said.

"I do not jest," Voroshilov stated bitterly. "The war took its toll on our country too. It depleted our natural resources and restricted our industrial capability. The non-Russian peoples in the U.S.S.R., the ones who always resented our superiority and our control, saw our weakness and decided the time was right to throw off their yoke. The Balts and the Mordivians, the Udmurts and the Mari, the Tartars and the Kirgiz, and many others rose in rebellion." He stopped, his face downcast.

"And what happened?" Hickok goaded him, stalling. The longer he could keep the lieutenant talking the further they would get from Washington and the more likely a chance would develop to make his play.

"We don't know," Voroshilov said sadly.

"You don't know?"

Voroshilov sighed. "During and right after the war, thousands of our troops were sent to America, to invade and conquer the capitalistic pigs. Our forces took over a large territory in the eastern U.S., but we did not have enough supplies and men to continue our push to the north and west of the Mississippi. Our drive through Alaska and Canada was stopped in British Columbia by the worst winter they had there in centuries. Over the decades, we have consolidated our domination of the American area we rule. Until thirty years ago, we maintained contact with the motherland. We knew the rebellion there had reached a critical stage. Then the shortwave broadcasts stopped. Cryptographic communications ceased. Every ship we sent to investigate failed to return. Our forces in America found themselves isolated, cut off from our motherland."

"Hold your horses," Hickok interjected. "You say you lost contact with Russia thirty years ago?"

"Yes."

Hickok pointed at the five soldiers on the opposite bench. "Then where the dickens did they come from? They sure don't look over thirty to me."

"They are not," Lieutenant Voroshilov replied. "Since we could not replenish our forces from the motherland, we've established a system of modified racial breeding."

"I don't follow," Hickok said.

"We impregnate selected American women," Lieutenant Voroshilov stated. "Their children are turned over to us for training and education. Our indoctrination is quite thorough. Russian history and values are stressed. Communism, of course, is exalted. The result you see before you. Soldiers every bit as Russian as if they had come from the U.S.S.R., and fluent in English and Russian."

"Where do you get these American women?" Hickok asked. "Do they volunteer?"

Voroshilov snickered. "They cooperate whether they want to or not."

Hickok ruminated on the revelations he'd received. The information explained a lot. Like, why the Russians had not invaded the Civilized Zone, why the Reds hadn't taken over the whole country. Simply because they lacked the manpower and the resources to achieve it. "How much of the country do you have under your thumb?" he ventured to ask.

Voroshilov reflected for a moment. "Let me see if I can remember the names of the states involved. New England we control," he said, "and southern New York, southern Pennsylvania, Maryland, New Jersey, southern Ohio, southern Indiana, portions of Illinois, Kentucky, Virginia, and West Virginia. We also have sections of North and South Carolina under our hegemony. We wanted to subjugate all of the Southeast, but the Southerners are a most hardy, independent lot. They resisted us every foot of the way and stopped our advance, leaving us the Northeast and a wide corridor in the middle of the East."

Hickok stared at Voroshilov. "I can't get over you tellin' me all of this."

Lieutenant Voroshilov grinned. "As I said before," he stated, "you won't live to pass it on. General Malenkov will not treat you so lightly the second time."

Hickok idly gazed at the five troopers on the other wooden bench, and at the sergeant, standing to the right of Voroshilov. The five had relaxed their guard and lowered their weapons, but the sergeant still covered him with an AK-47. He needed to stall some more, and hope he had a chance to go for his Colts. "You said there were several reasons why you're not takin' me straight back to Washington," he reminded the lieutenant.

Voroshilov nodded. "Time is of the essence. We must reach your vehicle as quickly as possible, before your people can remove it."

"You still think you can tote the SEAL to Washington with this contraption?" Hickok smacked the metal side of the copter.

"Easily," Lieutenant Voroshilov bragged. "We will dig a small trench under your vehicle, and then slide our sling underneath. Once the sling is secured, our helicopter will lift the vehicle into the air and transport it to General Malenkov."

Hickok thoughtfully chewed on his lower lip. If the Reds could do what they claimed, it would be a piece of cake to lift the SEAL into the air, then lower it again on its wheels. Hmmmm.

Lieutenant Voroshilov stood. "I must rejoin our pilot. You will be removed at our first refueling stop and held there until our return trip. We will pick you up and carry you to Washington for your rendezvous with General Malenkov and the KGB."

"Do you mind if I take off this uniform?" Hickok asked. "I've got my buckskins on under it, and I'm sweatin' to beat the band."

"As you wish," Lieutenant Voroshilov graciously offered.

Hickok started to tug on the uniform shirt.

Lieutenant Voroshilov turned to the sergeant. "Did you find any weapons on him when you searched him?"

The sergeant blinked twice, then cleared his throat. "We did not search him," he confessed. "He did not appear to be armed—"

CAPITAL RUN

With a sinking feeling in his gut, Lieutenant Voroshilov spun, hoping his premonition was inaccurate. Instead, he saw his worst fear realized.

Hickok had pulled the uniform shirt from his pants, exposing his buckskins. And also exposing the Colt Python revolvers tucked in his belt. But even as the uniform shirt came clear, his hands streaked to the pearl-handled Magnums, his draw an invisible blur.

The sergeant awoke to the danger first, and aimed his AK-47 at the gunman's head.

Hickok was already on the move, rising and stepping to the left, putting a few extra feet between Voroshilov and himself. His right Python boomed, and the sergeant's face acquired a new hole directly between the eyes.

The sergeant was thrown backward into a pile of crates by the impact.

Lieutenant Voroshilov went for his pistol, his arms seemingly moving at a snail's pace compared to the gunfighter's.

Hickok crouched and whirled, the Colts held at waist level, his elbows against his waist, and they thundered simultaneously.

Two of the five soldiers on the opposite bench were slammed into the wall of the craft, their brains exploding from their heads in a spray of red and pink flesh.

The remaining three were bringing their AK-47's to bear.

Hickok's next three shots sounded as one, his aim unerring, going for the head as he invariably did.

One after the other, the three Red soldiers died, each shot in the forehead, each astonished by the speed of their adversary, each overcome by their own sluggishness.

Lieuteant Voroshilov, in the process of drawing his automatic, realized the futility of the attempt and darted forward instead, his arms outstretched.

Hickok pivoted to confront the lieutenant, and his

fingers were beginning to squeeze the Python triggers when he thought better of the notion. He allowed himself to be tackled, carried to the hard floor of the cargo bay by Voroshilov's rush, his arms pinned to his sides.

Lieutenant Voroshilov tried to knee the gunman in the groin, but missed.

Hickok grinned, then rammed his forehead into Voroshilov's mouth.

Lieutenant Voroshilov was jolted by the savage blow; his head rocked back and his teeth jammed together. For the briefest instant, his vision swam, his senses staggered. When they cleared, he discovered the gunman standing over him, the barrels of the Pythons centimeters from his face.

"Piece of cake," Hickok quipped. He cocked the Colts. "Don't move! Don't even blink!"

Lieutenant Voroshilov froze in place.

Hickok backed up a step and glanced toward the door. Had the pilot heard the gunfire? Maybe not. The twin rotors on the copter were making a heck of a lot of noise. On the other hand . . .

Hickok stared at Voroshilov. "On your feet! Real slow! Hands in the air!"

Lieutenant Voroshilov complied.

"We're gonna walk up to the pilot," Hickok directed him.

Voroshilov licked his dry lips. "He will see us coming and lock the cockpit."

"You'd best hope he doesn't," Hickok warned, "or you'll be gaining some weight right quick." He paused. "How much do you figure a couple of slugs would weigh?"

Lieutenant Voroshilov swallowed. Hard. "What do you propose to do?"

"I don't propose nothin'," Hickok retorted. "I'm plain doin' it! You're gonna fly me to the SEAL."

"You're crazy! We'll never make it. You will be

caught," Lieutenant Voroshilov said.

"No I won't," Hickok disagreed. "All I have to do is stay out of sight when you land to refuel. There's no need for any of you to be getting off the helicopter. You'll land, refuel, and take off again without letting anyone else on board."

"Ground control will become suspicious," Voroshilov stated. "There are papers to sign—"

"Tell 'em you're in a big hurry," Hickok instructed him. "Mention General Malenkov. That ought to make 'em listen."

"It won't work," Lieutenant Voroshilov declared.

Hickok's voice lowered to an angry growl. "You best pray it does work, or you'll be the first to go."

Lieutenant Voroshilov gazed at his fallen comrades. He thought of the disgrace he had suffered, the shame heaped on his name and career. If he lived, he would be demoted. Or worse, sentenced to hard labor in one of the concentration camps. Or even executed. The honorable course would be to compel the gunman to shoot him now, to end his life before his failure was discovered. If he died now, he would be hailed as a hero whose death was a tribute to the Party and the State. He looked at the gleaming barrels of the Pythons, and couldn't bring himself to make the necessary move, to try and jump the gunman. He wasn't a coward, but he didn't want to die.

"What's it gonna be?" Hickok demanded. "You either do as I say, or I'll ventilate your eyeballs."

Lieutenant Voroshilov took a deep breath. "I will do as you say."

"No tricks," Hickok warned.

"No tricks."

"And do all your talkin' in English," Hickok ordered him. "Now that I know your men can speak both languages, there's no risk involved and I'll understand everything you say."

Lieutenant Voroshilov frowned. Who would have

believed it? Looking at the blond gunman's inane, carefree grin and hearing his ridiculous Western slang, who would believe he was so competent a fighter?

"Let's mosey on up to the cockpit," Hickok said.

Voroshilov hesitated.

"Something wrong?" Hickok asked.

"Are there many like you?" Lieutenant Voroshilov asked. "Where you come from, I mean."

"A whole passel of 'em," Hickok said. "Why?"

"Oh, nothing," Lieuteant Voroshilov said as he headed forward, carefully passing the gunman. "But if there had been more like you a century ago, America would still be free."

Hickok laughed. "I ain't nothin' special."

"That's what you think," Lieutenant Voroshilov said, complimenting his enemy.

21

They emerged from the bowels of the library into the fresh air and bright light of day in an alley due west of the building.

"You know St. Louis better than we do," Blade said to Lex. "You've got to lead us out of the city. Stick to the alleys and back streets. We don't want to run into any more Leather Knights."

"I'll do my best," Lex promised. She led off, Rikki at her side.

Blade followed them, covering their flanks, constantly scanning to the rear. Amazingly, the expected counterattack hadn't materialized. They hadn't seen or heard a single Knight during their exit from the library.

Why not?

The rest of the Leather Knights undoubtedly were alerted to the debacle in the pit room. At least one of the Knights in the room at the time had survived and vanished.

So where the hell were they?

If the Leather Knights hadn't appeared, there must be a good reason. But what? Were the Knights afraid? It hardly seemed likely since they numbered in the hundreds. Perhaps many of the Knights were in other sections of the city, but there had to be enough in the immediate vicinity to overwhelm the two Warriors and the defector. Yet they hadn't attacked. Were the Knights wary of attempting to corner their former prisoners in the narrow confines of the underground hallways? Or, as sounded reasonable, were the Knights reluctant to pursue the trio through the labyrinth under the library for fear they would lose their captives in the maze? If that was the case, and if he were a Leather Knight, what would he do next?

The answer was so obvious, Blade stopped as if stunned by a physical blow.

There was only one possible recourse! To cover every exit from the library and wait for them to come forth.

Rikki and Lex had reached the mouth of the alley and moved into the street beyond.

Blade ran toward them. "Rikki!"

He was too late.

Hidden in the buildings on every side, over two dozen Leather Knights rose from concealment, some in windows, others in doorways, some hiding behind gutted cars on piles of trash.

"Now!" a sister shouted.

The Leather Knights opened fire.

Startled by the ambush, Lex still managed to raise her rifle and blast a stud in a nearby window. Then her left shoulder was jarred, and the rifle flew from her hands as she started to fall.

Rikki reached her side in the next instant, ignoring the hail of lead raining all around him. He placed his left arm around her waist and lifted, supporting her weight as he hurried to the alley, knowing he wouldn't reach its cover without aid.

Blade burst from the alley with the Commando leveled. He swept the surrounding buildings with a devastating spray of bullets.

Sisters and studs screamed as they were hit, or ducked from sight to escape the giant's onslaught.

Blade retreated into the alley.

Rikki was holding Lex in his arms. A bright red circle had formed on Lex's left shoulder and there was a hole in her vest.

"Lex?" Blade asked.

Lexine, although pale, was game. "I'm fine," she told Blade. "Tell this yoyo to stop worrying about me."

Rikki gently eased her onto the ground. "Stay put," he advised her. "We will attend to the Knights."

Blade leaned against the west wall and eased to the corner. There was a lot of commotion from every nearby building. The Knights were reorganizing.

Rikki joined him. "Any orders?" he asked.

"If they rush us," Blade said, "we'll never hold them."

"We could reenter the library," Rikki recommended.

Blade shook his head. "That could be what they want us to do. Once we're inside, they'll close off the alley and have us bottled up inside."

"Then what?" Rikki inquired. "Do you want me to take them one by one?"

"If it was dark you could do it," Blade said. "But they'd spot you in broad daylight."

"I'd get a few," Rikki vowed.

"True," Blade agreed. "But I need you here. Lex needs you here."

Rikki glanced at the redhead. "I've become quite . . . fond . . . of her," he said in a soft tone.

"I've noticed."

"I've never felt this way before," Rikki declared.

"I know."

Beyond the alley, there was the rattle of a tin can.

Blade looked behind him. There was an eight-foot wall at the far end of the alley. Piles of garbage and debris were scattered everywhere. The stench was awful. If the three of them could reach that wall—

There was a loud clanking outside the alley.

"What are they doing?" Rikki inquired.

Blade risked a hasty peek.

Leather Knights were advancing on the mouth of the alley from both directions. To his right, four studs were pushing a wooden cart laden with metal trash cans filled to the brim with trash. Two sisters were carrying oddly shaped sticks or branches near the cart.

No!

They weren't sticks or branches!

They were torches!

Blade glanced at Rikki. "They plan to smoke us out. If we try to make a break for it, they'll cut us down in a crossfire."

"We can't stay here," Rikki said.

"I know." Blade scrutinized the buildings lining the street across from the alley. Knights weren't in evidence, but that didn't mean a thing.

Lex moaned.

Blade placed his right hand on Rikki's shoulder. "You'll have to hold them while I get Lex over the wall." He nodded toward the far end of the alley.

"I will hold them," Rikki pledged.

"They'll try and rush us," Blade guessed. "Try and shove a cart in here filled with burning trash, hoping the flames will spread and force us from cover. If you can hold them until I have Lex safe, I'll cover you from the wall until you reach us. Fair enough?"

"Sounds okay to me," Rikki said. He looked at Lex, clutching her shoulder in agony but not complaining. "Take good care of her. If something should happen to me . . . insure she reaches the Home safely."

"I will," Blade promised. "Here. Use the Commando."

"And what will you cover me with? Your Bowies?" Rikki grinned. "Get going."

Blade ran to Lex, slung the Commando over his right shoulder, and knelt. "Hold on tight," he cautioned her.

Lex opened her eyes. "Where are you taking me?"

"Out of here." Blade lifted her into his arms.

"I won't leave Rikki," Lex stated.

"You have no choice," Blade responded, and jogged toward the wall 40 yards away.

"Rikki!" Lex yelled.

Rikki smiled and waved, then flattened against the west wall. His sensitive nostrils detected the acrid scent of smoke.

It would be soon.

Blade and Lex were 20 yards off, Blade negotiating the trash and garbage as he threaded a route to the wall.

Rikki held his katana in front of him, calming his emotions. He had to shut Lex from his mind, to submerge his feelings for her and concentrate his total energy on the matter at hand.

Smoke drifted past the alley entrance.

It would be very soon.

Rikki emptied his mind of every distraction, focusing on the katana, wedding his instincts to the blade. He would buy Blade and Lex the precious time they needed, even at the expense of his own life.

"Do it!" a sister yelled from outside the alley.

There was a sudden clanking and rattling, and the Leather Knights swarmed toward the alley. The four studs pushing the cart were in the lead, the contents of the trash cans already ablaze, pouring whitish gray smoke into the air, obscuring the cart and the nearest Knights.

Rikki squatted, his eyes on the alley mouth.

The Leather Knights reached the alley, and for a moment they hesitated, their assault halted by a momentary confusion. Blinded by the dense smoke issuing from the cart, their confusion was confounded by all of them endeavoring to enter the alley at once. Unable to see their foes, they balked, and in so doing gave Rikki-Tikki-Tavi the advantage he needed.

Rikki plunged into their midst, holding his breath to minimize the effects of the odoriferous smoke. Wherever he saw a shape or shadow in the smoke, he struck. His katana cleaved to the left and the right, hacking limbs and tearing torsos.

Those Leather Knights at the forefront of the charge bore the brunt of the carnage. Prevented from firing by the density of their mad rush, they tried to retreat but were blocked by those behind them. The Knights in the rear, unaware of the clash because they couldn't see through the smoke, shoved those in front. Those in the lead, hearing the screams and shrieks of the wounded and dying and glimpsing a swirling figure in black, pushed against those in back.

Chaos reigned.

A lone stud with a Winchester appeared in the smoke, and Rikki slashed him across the neck.

The stud toppled backward from view.

Rikki saw a sister near the wooden cart, silhouetted by the red and orange flames, and he impaled her on the point of his sword. She gasped and grabbed the blade with her left hand, losing her fingers in the bargain.

"Damn you!" she defiantly cried as she expired.

Rikki crouched, his katana at the ready. Surely this was enough? Blade should have reached the wall by now! He picked his way over the bodies and through the smoke until he was in the alley. Gray tendrils drifted above the garbage and trash, obscuring the far wall. He hastened after Blade and Lex.

"Hold it, sucker!"

Rikki twirled, the katana extended.

It was the one called Erika, her portly features smeared with dirt, her leather garments begrimed a shade of brown. She held a shotgun in her hands, aimed at the man in black. Her eyes betrayed a maniacal quality, evidence of a personality on the brink of insanity. "You ain't going nowhere!" she barked.

Rikki stared at her fingers, waiting for the telltale flexing indicating she was going to pull the trigger.

"You thought you had me!" Erika cackled. "You and that big son of a bitch! Threw me into the pit! But I was too smart for the both of you! Grotto went after Terza, and I ducked into the hole connecting the pit to the sewers. I saw what it did to Terza!" Erika shuddered. "I stayed hid until after you left. Then some of the Knights showed up, and they tossed a rope to me." She laughed. "It was my idea to wait for you out here. I knew it'd take you a while to make it out." She tittered. "Pretty sharp, aren't I, lover boy?"

Rikki calculated five feet separated him from the crazed woman.

Erika raised the shotgun. "I'm going to enjoy this!" she declared, gloating, relishing her impending triumph. "Almost as much as I'll enjoy being the new leader of the Leather Knights!"

The street beyond the alley was quiet; the Knights apparently had retreated, abandoning their cart. Smoke continued to float into the alley.

"Any last words?" Erika baited Rikki.

A cloud of smoke drifted over Erika, enshrouding her head and shoulders in a mantle of gray. She coughed, recovered, and squeezed the trigger.

And missed.

Rikki threw his lean body to the left as the shotgun discharged. Her shot blew apart a pile of trash to the rear of where he had been standing just a moment earlier. Before she could fire again, his right arm swept back, then forward, holding the hilt of the katana, hurling the sword like he would a spear.

Erika, immersed in the suffocating smoke, experienced a burning sensation in her chest and glanced down. She released the shotgun and doubled over as the first waves of pain struck. "No!" she wailed. "No! No! No!" She dropped to the ground, her hands on the hilt, scowling in excruciating agony. A black foot appeared in her line of vision and she looked up, squinting.

The man in black was in a peculiar stance, his right hand rigid, the fingers firm and compact. "Yes," he said, and the right hand chopped downward.

22

"I don't believe it!" Blade exclaimed.

"I believe it," Rikki stated, grinning.

"I don't get it," Lex chimed in, gingerly adjusting the makeshift bandage on her left shoulder.

Directly ahead, parked in the center of the highway, upright, intact, was the SEAL. About 20 yards past the SEAL, also parked in the middle of the road, was an enormous Red helicopter. To the right of the SEAL, at the side of the highway, were two men in uniform, seated, propped against one another back-to-back, their wrists and ankles securely bound with rope.

"Is that your friend?" Lex asked Rikki.

"That's our friend," Rikki answered.

He was grinning from ear to ear, leaning on the SEAL's grill, his Colt Pythons tucked under his belt, his Henry cradled loosely in his buckskins clad arms.

"Howdy!" Hickok greeted them as they approached.

Blade, stupefied, pointed at the pair in uniform and the helicopter. "Who? How? Where?"

Hickok winked at Rikki, then turned a somber expression to Blade. "You always did have a way with words, pard."

Blade found his voice. "How in the world did you manage this?"

"It was a piece of cake," Hickok replied.

Blade stared at the helicopter. "Where did that come from?"

"Washington," Hickok modestly responded.

"Washington? Washington, D.C.?" Blade and Rikki exchanged astonished glances.

"Yep."

"I want a full report," Blade told the gunman.

Hickok yawned and shrugged. "I figured we'd need some help gettin' our buggy on its tires again, so I moseyed to Washington and asked the Reds if they would lend us a hand. Well, sure enough, they obliged. And here I am. The SEAL checks out okay. We can leave whenever you're ready, pard, unless you reckon you'd rather fly to our Home in the copter."

Blade shook his head in bewilderment. "Knowing you, there has to be more to it than that. I want a detailed report on our trip back."

"You'll get it," Hickok promised. He gazed at Rikki. "Is the lady with you?"

"This is Lex," Rikki introduced her.

"I've heard a lot about you the past two days," Lex said.

Hickok stepped up to her and offered his right hand. "Any friend of Rikki's is a pard of mine. Pleased to meet you."

Lex shook. "Likewise. I can't wait to meet your wife. Rikki told me you're married to a lovely woman."

"I think so," Hickok said. "She has the looks and I've got the brains. We're quite a combo."

"You have the brains?" Rikki repeated skeptically.

Hickok ignored the barb. He looked at Blade. "So where the blazes have you been?"

"We ran into a spot of trouble," Blade replied. "Spent the last two days sneaking out of St. Louis." He paused, suddenly feeling extremely fatigued. "I'll fill you in on the way to the Home."

"We have a heap to talk about," Hickok admitted.

"I'm ready to leave now," Lex stated eagerly.

"What about them?" Rikki inquired, indicating the

two prisoners and the helicopter.

"I have an idea," Hickok mentioned. "We could use our rocket launcher on the helicopter," he suggested, "and those two vermin can fend for themselves. They can't tell us much I don't already know."

Blade reflected for a minute. "We don't want to leave the helicopter in enemy hands, so destroying it is our only option. As for the two soldiers," he said, then paused, studying them. "We don't have time to interrogate them here. The Leather Knights could show up in force at any moment. And I can't see lugging them back to the Home in the SEAL. It's too far, and we'd be too crowded. Hickok's right. We'll do as he suggests."

"Hickok is right?" Rikki asked in mock amazement. "Remind me to tell Geronimo about this when we reach the Home. He'll never believe you said that."

The gunman pretended to glare at the martial artist. "What did you do? Pick up a sense of humor in St. Louis?"

Lex took Rikki's right hand in hers. "He picked up more than a sense of humor," she said proudly.

"Oh, no." Hickok looked at Rikki. "Does this mean we're gonna have another wedding soon?"

Rikki shrugged. "If the Spirit so guides us."

Hickok frowned and shook his head.

"What's the matter with you?" Blade asked. "What's wrong with Rikki getting married? You and I are married, you know."

"It's just a mite sad to see another good man bite the dust," Hickok quipped. "Another Warrior who'll come down with a bad case of dishpan hands."

"Let's get out of here," Blade declared, "before the Leather Knights catch up with us."

"You three look tuckered out," Hickok said. "I'll drive."

Blade sighed. "Just when I thought I was safe . . ."

About the Author

Dave Robbins was raised in southeastern Pennsylvania, amidst dense forests and rolling farm fields. At seventeen, he enlisted in the Armed Forces and, after serving overseas, returned to travel through America. He currently resides near the majestic splendor of the Rocky Mountains. A happily married family man, an outdoorsman, writer, and broadcaster, Robbins is acquiring a devoted core of readers who enjoy his finely crafted tales of adventure, romance, mystery and excitement. Collect every one from Leisure Books.